"Another winner from Kristin Dearborn, *Whispers* is full of monsters and mayhem, madness and paranoia, but also boldly-realized characters who live and breathe and feel like flesh-and-blood. Highly recommended . . . now bring on Dearborn's next one!"

James Newman, author of *Odd Man Out, Animosity, Ugly as Sin*

"Dripping with dread, charged with suspicion and betrayal, terrifying in its otherworldly loss of human agency and control—*Whispers* ranks among horror maven Dearborn's best and most unsettling works to date. It's always cause for celebration when Kristin Dearborn unleashes a fresh nightmare and this is no exception."

Ed Kurtz, author of *The Rib From Which I remake The World, Nausea*

WHISPERS

INSPIRED BY H.P. LOVECRAFT'S "THE WHISPERER IN DARKNESS"

by

Kristin Dearborn

Copyright Kristin Dearborn 2016

Front Cover by Raven Daegmorgan

Graphic Design by Kenneth W. Cain

Published by Lovecraft eZine Press

Formatting by Kenneth W. Cain

FOREWARD

by Daniel Mills

The whole matter began, so far as I am concerned, with the historic and unprecedented Vermont floods of November 3, 1927.

—HP Lovecraft, "The Whisperer in Darkness"

Lovecraft first visited Vermont in the summer of 1927, three months before the floods of November 2-4. This first trip to the state was brief but nonetheless affected him deeply, as later detailed in his essay "Vermont: A First Impression," where he writes of "alluring valleys," "green slopes," and of "little domed hills" behind which "time has lost itself... and around us stretch only the flowering waves of faery."

In 1928, Lovecraft returned to Vermont. This time he spent two weeks with friends near Brattleboro and observed first-hand the damage caused by the previous year's flooding, which had devastated the region's "ribbons of rutted whiteness" and "old wooden bridges" and resulted in the deaths of 85 Vermonters.

"The Whisperer in Darkness" (1931) opens with an account of the 1927 flood—no doubt inspired by Lovecraft's 1928 visit to the state—and of mysterious "things found floating in some of the swollen rivers." Later our narrator Wilmarth is obliged to travel to Vermont to visit the folklorist Henry Akeley. In describing the "little domed hills" of the Connecticut River Valley, Lovecraft recycles elements of his earlier essay but here the rapturous beauty of the landscape is suffused with an ancient menace.

There were awesome sweeps of vivid valley where great cliffs rose... gorges where untamed streams leaped, bearing down toward the river the unimagined secrets of a thousand pathless peaks. Branching away now and then were narrow, half-concealed roads that bored their way through solid, luxuriant masses of forest among whose primal trees whole armies of elemental spirits might well lurk...

However, this description of "luxuriant masses of forest" populated by "primal trees" is not entirely accurate. By 1928 much of Vermont's forestland had been clear-cut not once but twice to support potash production, pasture creation, farming, and logging, so that the state was probably close to 70%

deforested by 1870. This, in turn, worsened soil erosion and hastened the decline of farming in the state. Population growth stagnated. Farms failed and were abandoned. Vacant houses slumped into their foundations and the surrounding woodlands went un-worked for decades, allowing the forests to rebound.

In "The Whisperer in Darkness" Lovecraft offers up awestruck descriptions of the Vermont landscape but fails to consider the true cost of that wild beauty as measured in human tragedy: by decades of poverty, squalor, and despair. What seemed to him an ancient wilderness in 1927-1928 was in fact a byproduct of more than 50 years of economic and agricultural decline. And if the Green Mountains of today appear similarly unspoiled it is only because the Vermonters of the past endured hardships beyond our imagining—hardships which continue to be shared by the state's rural communities. In April 2014, an article entitled "The New Face of Heroin" appeared in *Rolling Stone* detailing the scope of the ongoing opiate crisis in Vermont. Many readers were shocked by the article's depiction of addiction, overdose, prostitution, and petty crime, while Vermonters, for the most part, were not.

Which brings us to Kristin Dearborn's *Whispers*. The whole matter begins, so far as Dearborn is concerned, with the historic floods of August 2011. On August 29th, 2011, Tropical Storm Irene swept through Vermont, washing away roads and bridges and swamping rural communities in a manner which recalled the 1927 flood. Three people were killed.

Dearborn sets *Whispers* in the immediate aftermath of Irene. In this way she consciously invokes the opening to Lovecraft's story even as her own vision of the Vermont landscape—informed by her many years in the state—differs markedly from that of the Gentleman from Providence. Here there are no "alluring valleys" or "green slopes" and yet Dearborn's depiction of the state is instantly recognizable to those of us who make our home in the Green Mountains.

In *Whispers*, the retired academic Sarah crosses paths with Neveah, a young addict who is on the run from her ex-boyfriend/pimp/dealer. At the beginning of the story, both women are trapped by circumstance into lives of quiet (and not so quiet) desperation much as they later become trapped—literally—in a cabin far from town. The setting is distinctly bleak. In place of "flowering waves of faery" there are instead failing cities, desolate hills, endless rainfall. Where Lovecraft saw wild beauty, Dearborn conjures instead a vision of a closing trap from which there can be no real escape—at least not in this world.

Near the end of "The Whisperer in Darkness," Akeley suggests that Wilmarth might travel with him to the planet Yuggoth, causing Wilmarth to recoil in horror. Later that night he flees the Akeley farmhouse after learning of his friend's true fate. It is a quintessentially Lovecraftian moment: Wilmarth is offered a glimpse of those "terrifying vistas of reality" referenced in "The Call of Cthulhu" and likewise runs from them, retreating not to a "new dark age" but rather to his old life in Arkham.

But, then, he is not a Vermonter. He has an Arkham to which he can return just as Lovecraft had the Providence he so dearly loved. For the protagonists of *Whispers* there is no such place of refuge. Sarah has only her life of isolation and loss lived out against an indifferent landscape while Neveah is similarly broken: her body ill-used, her addiction consuming. Lovecraft writes eloquently of the fear of the unknown, but in *Whispers*, the human world is shown to be every bit as horrifying as "the dark universe yawning, where the black planets roll without aim…without knowledge or luster or name."

Black stars are rolling in the skies over Kristin Dearborn's Vermont. To the characters of *Whispers* they offer namelessness, darkness, forgetting—and to some, perhaps, the only deliverance they will ever know.

1 – HORROR MOVIE OR A PORNO

Sarah knew she shouldn't pick up the hitchhiker. Rain buffeted the car and the afternoon sky closed in, a dismal gray. Thunder rumbled, echoing around the mountains before petering off, followed by a painfully bright flash of lighting.

The girl wore skinny jeans and an unseasonably light jacket over a white tank top. Even from here, Sarah could see her black bra under her soaked and skin-tight shirt. Long dark hair clung to her face and shoulders. Her eyes were black from pooling mascara and eyeliner.

She couldn't possibly be from around here. She couldn't be a threat, just a girl who needed a ride.

Sarah wondered why she was headed up into the mountains.

She looked back at the two dogs in the back seat. "You'll tell me if it's a bad idea, right?" They wagged at her and smiled their doggy smiles.

Sarah pulled over, putting her hazards on. She likely wouldn't see anyone else out here this afternoon, but if someone did come up behind her, she didn't want to take any chances.

The girl was hot. She remembered some movie that pointed out this was how both horror movies and pornos begin. For Sarah, the horror movie had started years ago.

"Where are you headed?" she called out the open window. The storm soaked the seat, and the dogs pushed past one another to get to her.

"East," the girl said, wiping at her streaking make up.

"There's not much east of here. Just the mountains. I can take you maybe ten miles." Sometimes there were hikers here, looking for rides. Sometimes there were people dressed as hikers, but Sarah knew their true purpose.

"Ten miles in this would be awesome."

The girl climbed in and the dogs said hello. She scratched them, patted them, and asked their names.

"They don't have names," Sarah said.

To her credit, the girl didn't say anything. Sarah turned the heater on in the car. Goosebumps stood out over the girl's pale skin. She kept her arms crossed across her chest, hugging the light jacket to her. Sarah thought of a hundred things to ask but they all seemed stupid, and before she knew it she was almost to her turn off. She'd let the girl out here, then go home.

Sarah put the hazards back on. "This is your stop."

"Hey listen... You don't... have a place I can crash, do you? Like, just until the storm is over?"

"No."

The girl's face fell. "You're sure? Any food?"

Sarah looked around the car. She didn't have anything. "I'm sorry, no."

The drive had taken the girl deeper into the green mountains. Her flimsy sneakers didn't look made for hiking, and she didn't carry a pack or water. What was she doing up here?

Sarah didn't say anything else because there wasn't anything else to say. The girl was pretty, she would probably dream about her tonight. It had been nice to talk to someone, to share space with someone, even for a little while.

Thunder crashed overhead and the girl flinched.

She couldn't come home with Sarah. It wouldn't work for either of them.

"Please. I have to get home."

The girl nodded. "Thanks for the ride." She got out, stepped into the downpour.

She closed the door. One of the dogs, a big brown mutt, spilled into her seat. Mostly Sarah tried to keep them in the back, but she didn't have the energy today. She left the girl huddled under a tree. The road was slick with fallen leaves. In sunlight, they would have made a rainbow, but the storm muted them and made them all look drab and brown.

She had plenty to time to get home before dark. She

wasn't going to be caught out here when the sun went down. The girl would be fine.

Less than a quarter mile from where she'd left her passenger she took a right, leaving the pavement behind and taking the Subaru down her rutted drive. There weren't many houses out this way. Hers was the highest on the hill, and if she'd cut the brush down this year, she'd have a beautiful view. She hadn't, though, and all she could see were the colors of autumn.

The driveway wended its way past boulders, following the path of a creek. In the storm, the stream was swollen and rushing, the normally clear water brown and frothy.

Things in the flood waters.

Hurricane Irene came in August, and with it had come... Best not to think about that now. Just like she ought not look for strange footprints in the fresh mud left by the storm. She brought the dogs inside, made sure all the doors were locked, pulled the shutters over all the windows, and started a fire in the woodstove. Her LED lanterns cast a cool glow that contrasted with the warmth of the fire. She lit the pilot on her propane stove and put a can of soup on to heat. She turned on classical music from her radio, and settled into a cozy chair by the fire. The shotgun was by her chair, loaded and easy to reach.

She watched the dogs. Five of them, big ones. They all lay by the woodstove, quiet, eyes closed. One dreamed, his hind legs twitching as he whimpered. When the dogs were calm there was nothing to fear. When they slept, so could she.

The heat from the fire warmed her, and one of the dogs snored softly. She let her eyes slip shut, feeling the softness of the chair, the old homemade quilt wrapped around her.

She wasn't sure how long the peace lasted. All five dogs exploded up, barking, claws scrabbling on wood floor, throw rugs scattered in their wake. They surged to the door, barking, tails waving expectantly.

Tails waving. When real danger came, they acted different, stiff and menacing. Now they were excited. She heard it, then, under the music, under the barking. The sound of someone knocking on her door.

2 – SHIVERS

Neveah didn't have to try to make herself look pathetic. Goosebumps covered her dimpled, soaked skin and the rain had flattened the hair on her head hours before. She couldn't stop shivering, her teeth clacking together from the cold. If she really tried, she could stop one or the other, but when she clamped her jaws together, shudders wracked her body. It all took too much energy to try.

Besides, she was hungry. Her stomach growled like an animal.

The gloomy gray afternoon had nearly transformed into black night, and the woods spooked her. She wanted to get inside.

This had to be where the woman had gone. It was the only driveway around, and the tire tracks in the driveway were fresh. She banged on the door again. Dogs barked inside, a whole lot more than the two that rode in the car with them earlier. Crazy dog lady, much?

At least Dean wouldn't find her out here. She longed for a hit like she'd never longed for anything, but she no longer had her bag. Her phone, her wallet—not that there was anything in it—the few pictures she had from the good old days. All gone.

It was liberating.

Except for losing her junk. That, she'd probably kill for.

Neveah saw a barn across the yard and decided if no one came to the door she could smash a window to get in there, at least until the storm was over.

It had seemed to make sense to cut through the mountains, to keep to the back roads on her way to Boston. She wasn't so sure now. She banged again on the door. This one seemed very solid compared to the flimsy trailer doors she was used to. She laid a hand on it. Willed it to open.

It didn't.

And then it did.

Neveah stared into the yawning barrel of a shotgun.

Dogs surged around the woman's legs. "I told you not to follow me. What are you doing here?"

Neveah started to cry. She started out faking it, but then it sort of came over her. She rode with it. "I'm trying to get to Boston and I don't have anywhere to stay. I don't have any food. I'm hungry and I'm so cold."

"You're a long way from Boston." The woman wasn't even looking at her, staring off over her shoulder, eyes darting around the darkening yard. It reminded her of Tito and the way he looked around since coming back from Afghanistan.

Neveah looked over her shoulder, but there wasn't anything out there. "Please. Just for a night?"

The dogs went quiet. Then one started to growl. Like the woman, it stared past Neveah, out into the darkness.

The woman's face lost all its color at once, and she grabbed for the dogs, shotgun forgotten. "Help me with them. Don't let them past. Come in."

Through her tears, Neveah reached for the dogs, corralling them into the house. She counted five of them, big, solid mixed breeds, mostly shades of brown and black, one black and white one. She recognized the two from the car ride amongst them.

The woman let Neveah in, then shut the door and barred it with a thick wooden board. Serious shit. She set the gun against the wall. The dogs watched the door, all rapt attention. The woman tore her stare away, and fixed on Neveah. "You want dry clothes? Something to eat?"

Duh. Still, Neveah remembered her manners. "Please."

Still watching the dogs, the woman disappeared into another room, came back with pilled brown sweatpants and a big University of Vermont sweatshirt.

"Do you have a bathroom?"

The woman pointed. Neveah started for it.

"Don't open the window."

"What? Why would I do that?"

"Just don't. Don't open the window."

"Okay." Neveah went, holding the sweats away from

her so she wouldn't get them wet. The toilet was weird looking, and the shower was tiny. No sink. Ick. This was one weird bitch. The window was completely shuttered. As she sat on the weird toilet, she wondered what would happen if she let the window open.

She didn't. She changed her clothes, hanging the wet ones over the shower bar. She took care not to look down and see the deep purple bruises. Her black thong and lacy bra looked particularly out of place. Fuck it. They'd be the best thrill her weirdo host had felt in a while.

She headed back out to the living room. The place was small, just one big, open room with a woodstove and a slate sink, a table, a chair and a futon. The doorway the woman got the clothes from was dark—likely her bedroom. Dead plants sat all around the cabin. Weird.

The dogs paced in front of the door, ears alert, tails down.

"What's out there?" she asked.

The woman jumped. "Nothing. Nothing's out there. I have canned food. You can pick what you want."

"Thanks."

The woman pointed at a door, which opened to a pantry. When she saw the cans of food, her stomach growled. She really was hungry. The guy in the pickup had bought her an Egg McMuffin and a coke this morning on their way out of Rutland. His kindness hadn't come free. She didn't care. She'd had to get out of Rutland, get away from Dean.

Neveah carried her selected can of Campbell's Chicken and Dumpling soup over to the woman at the woodstove.

"I can—"

The woman took it from her, and used an attachment on her Swiss Army knife to open it. She dumped it in a beat-up pot, and set it atop the woodstove.

"What's your name?" Neveah asked.

"We're not friends."

"I know. I just..." Neveah let her voice trailed off. She stood, totally awkward. This wasn't going at all how she'd planned. Maybe she'd be better off out in the storm.

A glance at the dogs, at the woman's shotgun, told her she was lucky she'd come in when she had, though. Something was out there, something the dogs and this woman didn't much care for. The idea sent a chill down her back, and she started to shiver again.

When the soup started to bubble, the woman thrust a spoon at her, and told her to eat from the pot. She did. It was in the running for best thing she'd ever eaten. She tried to pace herself, tried not to burn herself, but it tasted so good, warming her from the inside and filling her belly. She ate everything in the pot, and when she was sure the woman wasn't looking, she ran her finger around the inside and licked it clean.

"You can wash it up in the sink."

She was too full and content to argue, so she did it. The woman had some hippy dippy dish soap made from nature that didn't have any dyes or poison or probably any real way to clean things in it. Neveah couldn't wait to be out of Vermont. Coming here might have been the worst thing that ever happened to her.

When she was done washing her dishes she sat down on the futon carefully, expecting the woman to yell at her about something.

"You want to sleep?" the woman asked.

It couldn't be more than seven or eight—Neveah couldn't see any clocks around. Still, she was tired.

"I don't know."

"You can go in my room. In the back."

Was this where the bitch got demanding? Neveah hadn't expected to get through this without having to pay the woman something, and she sure as fuck didn't have any money.

"Um, I don't want to, like, take your bed or something."

"I'm not going to sleep in it. I have to stay out here."

"Why?"

The woman glared at her.

"You're sure?"

The woman turned her attention back to the door and the dogs.

Whatever. If she went in the bedroom, it had to be less weird in there, right? Neveah stood and started across the room.

"Here, take one of the lanterns. And don't open any of the windows. No matter what you hear."

Neveah reached for the lantern.

"Do you understand me?"

"Yeah, don't open the windows. I get it. Is there, like, a bear out there or something?"

"No. I wish it was a bear out there. Go to sleep. When it's light out, I'll take you to Brattleboro."

That was pretty sweet, she hadn't hoped to get so far. "Wow, thanks."

"Don't thank me. Just don't open the window."

"Got it." Neveah headed back into the bedroom, and paused in the doorway. "You're really not going to sleep in here?"

"No."

She closed the door—another solid, wooden door. There was even a little latch. It wouldn't keep someone out if they kicked the door in, but it would keep the door closed and the woman wouldn't be able to just come in. She latched it, feeling a gush of relief. When was the last time she'd been locked in somewhere, alone and safe?

She thought of Dean again, and felt a lump in her throat. She'd be free of him when she got to Boston. She'd look up Hunter and crash with him until... Until something.

The bedroom was as simple as the rest of the house, just a bed and a bookcase. The bed was unmade, with mauve flannel sheets. They looked really comfortable. So much nicer than the bed in the Rutland motel she'd been staying in. She got into bed and stared at the ceiling for a bit, then realized she couldn't sleep yet. The tiredness that she felt plagued her body more than her mind. She got out of the bed and walked over to the bookcase. Lots of feminist textbook-looking books, some books on Vermont folklore, and, the bottom row, some science fiction and fantasy paperbacks.

Neveah looked around as though someone might see her picking up a book. She couldn't remember the last time she'd read, well, anything. Probably junior year of high school. She chose based on the writing on the spine, *Something Wicked This Way Comes* in curved, menacing letters.

She returned to bed with the book. A photograph fell out, an image of her reluctant host, much younger, with another woman. Big surprise there. They had their arms around each other, and smiled for the camera. A little girl stood in front of them. A family picture. The backdrop was a wide sandy beach and a blue ocean and sky that had likely been bright once, but the photo had faded over time. Someone had written 1997 on the back in ballpoint pen. Neveah had been five when the photo was taken. The girl in the picture was probably a year or two older than she was. Weird. Where was the family now? The woman seemed too crazy to have anyone in her life.

Neveah tucked the photo back into the book and started to read. She even started to doze off.
Until the dogs started barking and growling, sounding like they were trying to raise the dead.

3 – FOOTPRINTS

Sarah found herself still awake when the sky turned pink in the east. She'd put peepholes in the shutters so she could see outside when she needed to. Red sky in morning, sailors take warning. Likely it was the remnants of last night's storm still lingering. The dogs dozed around her, furry puddles. Her eyes felt like sandpaper, and her stomach was sour from lack of sleep.

They had been outside last night. They'd kept the dogs up, pacing and growling.

She kept looking at the closed bedroom door. If she opened it, would she find the girl had opened a window in the night? It was far too easy to imagine finding one of *them* curled in her bed instead of the little hitchhiker. *Never should have let the girl in.* But what choice had she had? Night had been falling. She didn't know what they would have done with the girl, but hikers and other people had gone missing from these woods for decades. It wouldn't have been good.

Sarah left the windows shuttered and tried the phone. The Comcast people had come and fixed the lines the previous week, warning her it was the last time. Something kept cutting the wires. "Bury them," she'd insisted, but they told her they wouldn't do it for one house out here. Same with the power company, though they'd stopped repairing her lines last month.

She'd bought a satellite phone, got satellite internet, but they were even better at disrupting those signals than they were at cutting the lines.

The sun crept up over the mountains, setting the dew on the tall grass outside to sparkle. She'd loved it here once.

The girl had slept long enough. She'd rouse her, get her out to the car, and they'd go. She could be back by one or two, do her shopping for the week today too, not tomorrow like she'd planned.

She tried to open the bedroom door, but found it latched.

Had the girl gone out the window in the night?

She knocked on her own door, wondering what she might find behind it. "Come on, get up. I'll take you to Brattleboro."

On the far side of the door, a mumble. A typical, sleepy teenage girl sound. For the first time since she'd met the girl, thoughts of her daughter edged in.

"Come on, let's go."

She pushed away the thoughts of Cassie. Cassie was safe, far, far away from here.

Sarah went into the bathroom to find the girl's skimpy underwear hanging from the shower curtain. She didn't like thinking of Cassie and looking at the lacy black bra and skimpy thong at the same time. She wondered if this was how straight mothers felt when they ogled younger men while thinking of their sons.

The girl in her bedroom looked of age, and besides, it wasn't like Sarah was going to do anything other than take her to Brattleboro.

She banged on the door again. "Let's go."

The dogs milled about and as she fed them, and the girl stumbled out of the bedroom looking sleepy and bedraggled.

"Your clothes aren't dry yet. If you want to keep the sweats, that's fine." If she was smart she would take them. It was October, too cold for the girl's flimsy jacket. It could snow up here any day now.

"'Kay."

"We'll get something to eat when we get there. Let's go."

The girl grabbed her damp clothes and wadded them up in the pocket of the sweatshirt.

Sarah selected two of the dogs to come with them. She picked the black and white female and a big tan male. She didn't want favorites—they weren't pets—but she really liked the tan dog. He was a big pit bull mix, even-tempered and friendly.

She silently told the remaining three dogs to watch the house. She locked the door behind her, and scanned the tree line. The sky promised to be blue once the sun was up.

"What's that?" the girl asked. Sarah's heart sprang into her throat. The girl pointed at the ground, at a strange shape in the mud.

"Nothing."

"It looks like... a claw print. Like a big bird or something?"

"Must have been a falling branch." Sarah unlocked the barn where she kept the Subaru parked, and slid open the big door.

"There's a bunch of them. Come look at these."

She ignored the girl and got in the car. Each and every time the engine started, she thanked her lucky stars. She let the dogs in the back, and they sat on the seats, looking out of back windows opaque with dried dog slobber.

"They really look like foot prints," the girl said, climbing in the car. Sarah just turned around and headed down her driveway. The rain hadn't been too unkind to it. A whole section had washed out during Irene. At least the remnants of last night's storm had left the driveway passable.

Had all of this really only been going on for fewer than two months? It almost made her dizzy to think how different her life had been before the storm. All around her, brilliant fall leaves brightened the early morning. She'd always loved the fall. Now, though, this year... She hoped the snow would slow them down.

"Are those tracks from what you're so scared of?" the girl asked.

Sarah almost went off the road. "I'm not scared," she said.

"Bullshit."

She glanced over at her passenger, keeping most of her energy on the car and the narrow, winding driveway. "You don't know what you're talking about."

"Whatever."

They drove on in silence. Sarah stopped at the end of her driveway, where she met the paved road. She looked both ways, even though she could count on one hand the number of cars she regularly saw out here. She turned right, continuing up the mountains, towards Brattleboro.

She didn't get far. A fallen tree barred the road.

"Fuck." The girl shrank in her seat.

Sarah maneuvered the car through a three-point turn in the narrow road to get herself turned around. "Rutland then. I'll take you there."

"No!"

Sarah couldn't remember the last time she'd seen such fear in someone's eyes.

"Anywhere but there. Can't we move the tree? Do you have, like, a chainsaw? Something?"

"You can get a bus in Rutland."

"I'm never going back there. And I can't go anywhere near the bus station. Especially not there."

"What about Bennington?"

"East. I have to go east."

"There's not another good way around the mountains." She racked her brain. Maybe she could head down towards Route 100.

It didn't matter. West of her driveway, another tree lay across the road. Sarah took deep, concerned breaths, irritated to see its presence calmed her passenger. She'd head back to the house, get her chainsaw. They'd go to Brattleboro after all.

She shoved away thoughts about *how* exactly two trees had managed to fall across the road leading away from her house, cutting off both directions. Yes, the weather was bad, and it was windy, but it was too neat. Too convenient.

They drove in silence a little while longer.

"What's your name?" the girl asked. "Since we're stuck together and all."

"We're not stuck together. We're going to go back to get my chainsaw, and we'll cut our way free. We'll be in Brattleboro by this afternoon."

"I'm Neveah."

Neveah. What kind of a name was Neveah? She hadn't wanted to know the girl's name. Like with the dogs, names made things personal. The girl was no longer "the hitchhiker she'd let spend the night", she was Neveah, a living person, with a past, and wants, and dreams.

"Sarah." She couldn't not offer up her own name.

"You don't look like a Sarah."

Instead of answering, Sarah turned the Subaru around again, then headed up the hill, down her driveway, along the stream. It was calmer today, not quite as brown. She parked by her shed and let the dogs out. The girl—Neveah—stepped out to play with them. Sarah wanted to tell her not to. They weren't pets.

But why shouldn't the girl and the dogs have some fun?

The barn window was smashed, her chainsaw pulled apart. The pieces appeared to be neatly removed, but she knew that when she put them all back together again, something would be missing. Something critical for the operation of the machine. It didn't even shock her any more.

She was trapped up here. Trapped with her hitchhiker. She never should have stopped for the girl. Somehow, in Sarah's head, this was all her fault, linked to her presence.

"My chainsaw is broken," she told Neveah.

"Can't you fix it?"

"I don't think so."

"That's cool. We'll just stay here until they get the roads taken care of." She rubbed the tan dog behind his ears. His eyes closed to slits. He laid his ears back, and tapped his tail on the gravel drive. "Isn't it kind of weird that there are trees down over the road on both sides of your driveway?"

Neveah's words made a lump in Sarah's throat. Yes, it was weird. Of course it was weird. Was the girl being facetious, or making a sincere observation? What did the girl know?

"Where did you come from?" Sarah asked.

"Nowhere."

Not the answer Sarah was looking for.

"Did you grow up here? Vermont?"

"No."

"Where?"

"We moved around a lot." The girl avoided eye contact, stared out at the trees. It was the tail end of foliage season, and the vibrant reds and oranges were beginning to shift to browns. Many of the branches were already bare.

"When did you come to Vermont?"

Neveah smiled at her, an insincere gesture of goodwill. "I'd rather not talk about it. I didn't have a great time here, and I'm looking forward to getting to Boston."

"Did someone tell you to come up here?"

Neveah put her hands up, defensive. "I know you've got some sort of paranoid thing going on, and that's fine. But I'm not a part of it."

Of course she'd say that. She wouldn't just fess up and admit it.

"How long do they usually take to get road crews out here, anyway?" she asked.

"No. You're not changing the subject. Did Asa Gardner tell you to come up here? Dave Cavender?"

"I've never heard of them."

"Did they tell you to watch for my car?"

Neveah backed away from her. "You're freaking me out."

"Yeah, well, I'm pretty freaked out myself."

"I think I'll take my chances walking to Brattleboro. Thanks for dinner and everything." The girl headed down the driveway.

Sarah's heart pounded. Surely Neveah would turn around, hearing the noise.

The best thing would be to let her go. She wasn't Sarah's problem. The things out here tended not to bother you unless you showed a little too much interest. Like taking pictures of their tracks. Trying to follow them. Or... other things Sarah had done.

4 – WE'LL SHOW YOU THE STARS

The bitch was clearly crazy. Neveah didn't know how she felt about the second tree being down. It kept her from being taken back to Rutland, sure, but it felt *wrong*. Like, those trees hadn't fallen on their own. At first the walk down the dirt driveway was pretty, the stream flashing clear and shallow over smooth stones. It made a churning, happy sound, and for a bit, it distracted her from her thoughts. It was nice to be someplace so quiet. No traffic sounds, no birds, just the wind in the trees and the water from the stream.

Neveah wasn't an outdoor girl. She didn't particularly care for nature, had never camped, never hiked, and never wanted to. With each step, she was too cold, too hungry, her feet hurt in her still-wet shoes, and holy shit did she need a fix. She could feel the pipe in her hands, could imagine every detail of herself lighting it and breathing the smoke in.

Nope. Just too-cold October mountain air.

Fuck.

She could score some in Boston, she knew. Which made it all the more important to get there. Her mouth was dry, and while she tried to ignore it at first, the sound of the water on the rocks dug into her brain like a worm or a needle. She stopped and went down to the stream, stepping right in with her sneakers.

Damn, the water was cold.

They were high up, right? So it wasn't like the water came through a toxic waste dump to get here, right? She cupped her hands and brought the water to her lips. Then, wet sneakers squishing, she went back on her way. On the road she made a right turn, up the hill. She easily climbed over the fallen tree. The road became more and more narrow, then all at once, the pavement stopped. The road was dirt.

Was this the right way?

She was following a fucking road. Of course it was the right way.

Neveah looked down at her wet sneakers to steady herself. Right next to her foot was a weird print like the ones in Sarah's yard. She dropped to one knee, eager for an excuse to stop. Placed her hand next to the thing. The print dwarfed her hand, had two claws in the front, one in the back.

A bird?

She looked up to the sky, visible between branches. She didn't see anything up there.

Neveah.

She froze and looked around. She'd heard her name. Someone whispered it, a buzzing, insectile whisper—but her name, clear as the blue autumn sky overhead.

"Sarah?"

Score some crystal with us, Neveah.

What? Her body felt electrified. Someone up here had some? And they were willing to share?

And they knew her name?

Once, Dean tried to dry out. It was funny. He'd wanted custody of his little girl, but her bitch mother wouldn't hear it. He said he'd just deal, wouldn't sample the product, and so he quit, cold turkey.

Neveah'd watched him sleep eleven or more hours a day, watched as he heard voices, saw things. He'd talked about shadow people, things slinking around the outside of his peripheral vision, hungry things, watching him.

It came down to Neveah to decide what to do with him when he started ranting and raving. Like, really ranting, a break from reality. The internet told her to take him to the ER, but she couldn't do that; how would he pay? And he'd never get his daughter back.

So she gave him a hit. And the shadow people melted away, and he went back to using and dealing and beating the ever loving shit out of her and... and all the other shitty things he did.

She started to cry.

This way, Neveah. Come light up. It's good stuff. Fly with us. We'll show you the stars.

Her mouth was dry again, and she knew—or she thought she knew—that the voices weren't real. The whispers swirled around her, coming from each dead brown leaf on each tree. They chanted her name and it made her think of chugging beers, of sucking cock, a false encouragement from people who say they're your friends but to whom you're nothing more than a spectacle.

Please, Neveah, we miss you.
We have so much to show you.
Come in to the woods with us, Neveah.
We have money and drugs and we'll take care of you.

Dean said he would take care of her. Look at where she was now. Beaten and bruised in the middle of the woods, wearing some old dyke's sweats. At least in Rutland she'd known where she was.

She dropped into a ball on the dirt road, amid the strange clawed tracks. The voices filled the road, switching out of English now to a guttural language she didn't understand. Spanish, maybe? Maybe Chinese? What the fuck did she know? She clapped her hands over her ears. Her breath forced itself from her lungs in rabid gasps, and her nose ran. She wanted to wipe away the snot and the tears, but then she'd have to pull her hands from her ears.

There really were things out there, because covering her ears helped.

Then it dawned on her. Sarah *must* have crystal, or she wouldn't be so paranoid. What else could explain the dogs, the shuttered windows, the constant sense of fear? Neveah pushed herself up to stand, faced down the hill, and ran.

Neveah, come back. We'll show you the stars.

No. She didn't want to see the stars. Didn't want to see any of it. When she came to the fallen tree, she tried to jump over it. She failed, crashing down on one knee and skinning it, a hot rush of blood pulling her out of her own head. Her palms were scraped and raw, rocks from the road embedded in them.

Deep breaths. It was all in her head. Just like it had been in Dean's head.

We'll show you the stars.

The insectile voice pushed in around her.

If you come with us, Neveah, Dean will never find you.

Something shifted in the forest, something pinkish—not human colored, more like the crayon color called salmon. It was out of tune with the colors of fall. Its weight caused a branch to snap, loud in the swaying trees.

The offer almost drew her in. If they could promise she would be safe from Dean...

But she thought of the buzzing nature of the voice. The footprints.

She ran.

5 – MISSING SOMETHING

Dean debated between brushing his teeth and not, like he did every time he woke up. The logic of "skipping them just the once" tended to win out, so "just the once" was more like six days a week.

Sierra appeared in the doorway, skimpy panties and a cropped T-shirt. "Someone's at the door," she mumbled. Sierra was a mumbler.

"Who is it?" he asked. He was awake enough to think about brushing, his teeth—or not—but not nearly awake enough to think about who might be at the door. He lit a cigarette.

"I don't know." She shrugged. "I didn't look. I just know someone is knocking."

Dean sighed, glanced at the clock and his pipe, and figured Marko must be early for his pickup.

"Can you go get some product ready?"

Sierra sighed and disappeared.

Dean pulled on a pair of shorts and a white t-shirt he'd only worn once. It didn't smell too bad. He headed out into the living room of the shitty little apartment.

Someone knocked again.

Dean opened the door, just a crack.

A man stood outside, standing a little too straight. Dean's hackles went up. He wore a flannel shirt and jeans, and his dark hair was a little long, over his ears. Big yellow work boots on his feet solidified the image that this was a native Vermonter.

"Yeah?" Dean asked.

"You Dean?"

"Depends who wants to know."

"Name's Asa. I hear you're missing something."

Missing something? He studied the Vermonter. Asa. He spoke carefully. "Not that I'm aware of."

"One of your girls ran out on you?"

Thoughts of Neveah rained down on him. His chest still burned where she'd raked her stupid claws across him. "What of her?"

"I know where she is."

He ground his teeth together. Willed his hands not to ball into fists. "How do you know?"

"I saw her. Saw her hitchhiking."

"So you know where she *was*."

"No, I know who picked her up, and who brought her home."

Dean laughed. Neveah was a hot little parasite who couldn't find herself responsible for her own lazy ass if she tried. In theory she'd be easy to find. Follow the trail of her marks.

"She's talking about calling the cops on you."

That made Dean pause. Sierra popped up at his shoulder, a plastic Hannaford bag in one hand. She'd put on a pair of shorts, but they were so short he wasn't sure why she'd bothered. Asa gawked at her. She curved into Dean. The girl knew how to give a show.

"She's going to the cops. Going to blow the lid on your operation." The man no longer looked at Dean. Sierra drank up all his attention.

"But you know where she is?"

Asa nodded.

Neveah *could* go to the cops. She could cop a plea, give him up in exchange for jail time. She might serve some, but the cops liked to get the bigger fish. She was a small fish. Dean let his imagination linger over what Stolz would do if Dean were pulled in and the cops found their way on to him. Dean was a bigger deal than Neveah, sure, but he wasn't at the top of this food chain.

"Has she already talked to the police?"

"I don't think so."

He'd already decided to let Sierra step up in her place. Neveah'd been difficult sometimes, sure, but her spunk made her a client favorite. He'd been waiting on Marko to come, then he'd been about ready to go out on the road to track Neveah down. This certainly saved him some time, if the man's intel was good.

"Why don't you come in?" Dean opened the door to admit Asa. Sierra stepped aside and let him pass.

6 – CRYSTAL

Sarah'd let the grass grow over most of what had been a beautiful green lawn. She didn't like being outside for the time it took to mow. *They* watched her when she came outside, and she didn't want to give them any more information about her than she could possibly help. She kept the area between the driveway and the house clear, and between the driveway and the shed. That was for safety reasons—if she needed to make a run for it, it was easier over cut grass than through the overgrowth.

Not that it mattered. If they were dropping trees outside so she couldn't leave, what did it matter? Where would she go? Certainly not into the forest. Plus soon it would start snowing, and it would all be moot. Would the plow trucks even do the roads this winter?

The two dogs outside with her lifted their heads down the driveway. No growling, no barking, just attention.

Sarah's first thought was of a deer—but that was silly. There wasn't much wildlife in these woods these days. She'd seen a raccoon dead on the road a week or so ago, and almost wept for the little life cut short.

She stared down the driveway, where sunny day turned dark in the shade of the trees. A big brindle pit mix took off down the driveway, and the black and white spotted dog went with her. Every so often she thought about naming them, but being her dog was dangerous work. These animals were tools, and it didn't do to think of them as anything more.

She started after them, calling "Dogs! Come here!" Not having names, not having much of a bond with her, they didn't heed her voice. They weren't there to obey, they were there to watch and stand guard.

She didn't need to train them to warn her when things

came in the night.

Picking up the shotgun resting against her stoop, she hurried after the dogs. Around a bend in the driveway, she found Neveah, running towards her. The girl caught up with her and wrapped her arms around her, falling on her, sobbing. The dogs circled and jumped up, curious to see what the fuss was about.

The girl left bloody hand prints on Sarah's sweatshirt.

"The shadow people are following me." Her words came in ragged pants, and she needed to wipe her nose. Sarah led her towards the cottage. "You have drugs, right? You have to. I need them. Please."

Sarah didn't say anything, just walked the girl into the little house, got her settled on the futon. Her skin felt hot and dry, and her lips were cracked.

"Need crystal."

"Who's Crystal?"

Neveah shook her head. "Crystal. Meth. Can I have some? I'll pay you back."

Ah. That explained it. The girl was in the throes of withdrawal. Relief gushed over Sarah—she worried Neveah'd seen something out on the road. It explained why the girl was so hungry and why she'd slept for so long. Once upon a time, Sarah had been a professor at the University of Vermont. She'd had a few students go through this before, one of whom dried out on her couch.

She ran her hand over the girl's hair. "Go to sleep."

"Too hot."

The sweatshirt, perfect after the soaking rain, was a little much for the warm autumn afternoon. "I'm sorry. Go to sleep."

Neveah did, tossing and turning on the futon. The sweatshirt rose up, and Sarah caught glimpses of deep purple bruises on her concave, pale stomach.

Under normal circumstances, being stuck in the woods outside the temptation to relapse would be the best thing possible for the girl. Not these woods though, and not now. Sarah left her to continue her maintenance of the cabin's fortifications.

***

While she was out, the dogs again stared off down the driveway, then hurried off in pursuit of some sound.

This time Sarah found her neighbor strolling down the drive. The dogs didn't rush to greet him, they gave him a wide berth, woofing at him, circling him. She carried the shotgun, half raised so Cavender would know she wasn't fucking around.

"What do you want?"

Cavender lived two miles down the hill from her, and had always been a model neighbor. After the flood however, his biologist wife had disappeared, and Cavender began acting suspiciously.

"Saw the tree down. Wanted to check in and make sure you were all right."

"I'm fine. You can go now."

"You're as good as trapped up here."

"Get off my land." She raised the gun up, just a little.

He raised his hands. "Try talking to them instead of shooting at them."

She pointed the shotgun square at her neighbor.

"I know about the little girl you got staying with you. You want to drag her into this mess?"

How? How did he know? It made her sick. Nothing was sacred, nothing was private. She pumped the gun—how many more warnings would he need? She wasn't going to shoot him unless he attacked her, but she couldn't think of another way to make him go. "It's not as though I can just drive her out of here."

"Send her with me. I can take her back to Rutland. Back to her home."

His words didn't sit right with her. Nothing he'd said for months sat right with her. Plus the girl very adamantly seemed to not want to go back to Rutland. And how did he know she came from there? Sarah herself didn't even know she came from there—she could assume it, but the girl had never came out and said it. How did they know?

They always knew.

Sarah backed away.

"I promise you," Cavender said, "life will be easier if you hand her over now. She's a complication you don't need."

Hand her over. Like she was a prize, a sack of cash, a MacGuffin. Sarah drew back and left Cavender in her driveway.

She knew he wouldn't hurt her—that was for *them* to do.

Back in the cabin, Neveah slept on the futon, the tan dog curled beside her on the floor. He watched Sarah with light eyes. He'd taken to the girl. How nice for both of them. The black and white dog nuzzled Sarah's hand and she pushed it away. It went and curled on the floor by the inert woodstove with a doggy sigh.

The morning rolled on to afternoon. Before the sun started to sink below the mountains, Sarah took two of the dogs down the driveway, past the footprints where she and Cavender had their conversation, and out onto the main roads to check the two trees trapping them in. Both were still there. Road crews hadn't come yet. Dammit.

She didn't like her neighbor's curiosity about the girl. He'd been interested in Sarah since his wife vanished, inviting her to dinner after dark, asking her to think about talking to *them*. No, no, and no. She wouldn't do any of those things. She couldn't imagine being alone with this man.

But she suspected that at any meeting, she wouldn't be alone with him for long.

Where had his wife gone? She didn't think they'd killed her, and that, somehow, made it worse.

Back in the cabin, Neveah sat on the futon, eyes wide and disoriented. "I didn't know where you went." Sleep thickened her voice.

"To the road to check on the trees. They're still there."

"We're safe here, right?"

"Of course." Sarah started her rituals, checking the shutters, bringing in firewood for the night, laying out enough batteries so none of the lanterns or flashlights would go dead. "Are you hungry?"

Neveah nodded. She stood and wobbled. It had been almost a day since the girl had eaten. Almost a day exactly since Sarah stopped to pick her up.

Part of Sarah, watching the girl select a can of cheeseburger stew, suspected if she hadn't picked the girl up, she would have passed through the mountains unmolested by now, on her way to Boston. It would have been a nasty night in the storm for sure, but the girl would have dried out today and been about her business.

Neveah ate, and Sarah prepared her own can of food,

the old standby of chicken noodle. She'd hoped to get to the store today, and regretted not having anything fresh on hand.

Outside, the sun set. Inside, the cheery glow of the fire in the woodstove lit the warm wood of the cabin. The dogs curled on the floor. Their peace meant everything was all right.

"I want to thank you for picking me up last night," Neveah said.

"No problem." Sarah stared down at her empty can, feeling suddenly awkward and gawky.

Neveah leaned in close. "I mean I really want to thank you."

When Sarah raised her eyes, Neveah was there, and their lips met. Neveah tasted like cheeseburger soup, but Sarah didn't care. For one beat, then two, then three, she let Neveah lead the kiss. Her lips were soft, sensual, her tongue inquisitive.

Then, with reluctance, Sarah pushed her away.

"I'm so sorry," Neveah said. "I don't know what I was thinking. I'm sorry. Can I, uh, take a shower?"

"Sure." Sarah's mouth was dry now, her lips feeling full and kissed. "Runs out of hot water fast, so make it quick."

"Thanks." She vanished into the bathroom and closed the door behind her.

"And keep the shutters closed!"

7 – HOSTS

Dean stopped in the little town of Wickenden, tucked in at the bottom of the foothills. The mountains loomed overhead in the darkness.

Asa, in the passenger seat, said, "You'll want to find a room here for the night."

"How far is she?"

"Maybe another hour."

"It's only eight. We can be there by nine. Element of surprise."

Asa smiled a knowing smile, one Dean didn't much care for. He'd made some cash off the man earlier in the day—Sierra's charms were too much for him, and he'd shelled out five hundred bucks for two hours with her. When they'd come back out of the bedroom, Asa wore a wide grin and Sierra had given Dean a nasty scowl. He hadn't had a chance to ask her what her problem was. He left her back in the apartment in Rutland. She had some other appointments tonight. She'd wanted to come, though. She'd never cared for Neveah, liked her even less now that the little cunt was a snitch and a thief.

"You don't want to be up in those hills in the dark."

"Or what?"

"Or lots of things. You could go off the road, get turned around and get lost. There's a whole lot of nothing up there. We'll do better in the morning. I know a place where you can let a room for the next few days."

Next few days? No. Dean wanted to get in, get his girl back, and get out.

Asa led him through a picturesque downtown, and advised him to park behind a building which housed both a mini cupcake boutique and a Laundromat. They headed up a set of rickety stairs on the outside of the building, and Asa knocked at an apartment door. Cheery curtains covered the window, and yellow light glowed inside.

A woman in her fifties or sixties opened the door. Her eyes were warm for Asa, but iced over when they fixed on Dean. He wasn't that bad to look at—shaved head, goatee, bulky Fubu jacket. His mother was half-Hispanic, and he had her dark skin and almost-black eyes. Rutland was cool, but any time he left, man, he got dirty looks as if he was fresh over the fences from Mexico. Vermont didn't have a lot of *persons of color*. In the city, he thought of himself as white. Perspective made a big difference.

"Christina, this is my friend Dean. Dean, this is Christina. She has a spare bedroom you can let."

"Naw, man. I'm good to stay at a motel."

"The motel closed for the season last week. Please, make yourself at home." She glared at Asa as she said it.

"Dean's missing property is up at the Sorrell Place."

Christina's eyes changed. "The hitchhiker?"

"She's a whore and a drug mule," Asa said.

Now Christina looked like a cat who'd eaten a canary. "I knew Sorrell wasn't as high and mighty as she likes to pretend."

"I don't think she knew what the girl was when she picked her up," Asa said.

"Tomorrow," Christina said. "We'll get the road cleared, and we'll go up there tomorrow."

8 – PARTITION

Neveah stepped into the bathroom, stripped, and turned the water on in the tiny shower. She let it get nice and hot before she ducked inside, then pulled the plastic curtain shut. She opened her mouth to the water and rinsed the taste of the kiss out. Bleh. Kissing women was so different than kissing men. Their lips were softer, seemed to understand better than a man's did.

It didn't mean she liked it.

Sarah had liked it. Neveah'd felt her desperation, especially in the moment when she'd pushed her away. She needed Sarah to keep her here, keep her safe, until the roads cleared up. Then she needed the ride to White River Junction. If she was lucky, she could get bus money, and could be where she needed to go in a couple of days.

If Neveah were going to go dyke, it wouldn't be with an old lesbian like Sarah. Maybe she'd been pretty once, but she had wrinkles all around her eyes, and her curly hair was streaked with grey. She was thick and large too, not fat, just big—wide hips, ample breasts, long stocky legs.

Neveah scrubbed herself. She'd done worse. It was all just a job. Everything in life was. An exchange of goods and or services. You had to realize that everyone had something they could trade, it was just a matter of how willing you were to give it up. When it had already been taken from you, some things you didn't protect as much. Long ago, Neveah had learned how to shut off a part of her brain and go somewhere else while her body was occupied. Drugs helped—they helped a lot—but she'd needed to be able to partition herself sober as well.

Neveah.

Her thoughts ran to a screeching halt and goosebumps

rose on her skin, despite still having some of the hot water left.

"Sarah?" It squeaked out, barely more than a whisper.

It would be just like the old dyke to slip in here to sneak a peek at her. Except her thought wasn't really fair, Sarah wouldn't do that.

Besides, it was the voice from outside. On the road. The one that spoke in a buzzing whisper, the way she'd imagine a cartoon fly or bee to talk. She imagined a six-foot tall bee outside the shuttered window and shivered. She thought of those footprints in the mud.

She rinsed herself, loath to put her face under the water. If *she* were going to attack someone in the shower, she'd do it when they had water and soap in their eyes.

Nothing attacked, but the bathroom sounded agonizingly quiet when she shut the water off. A drip continued, and each drop of water sounded like a thunderclap as it landed in the shower.

Open the window, Neveah.

She wrapped the towel around herself. It was small and scratchy, which made sense because Sarah didn't seem like she would have a dryer. She rubbed at herself, then got into her own clothes.

Dean's on his way. If you come with us tonight, he'll never know where you are.

From the living room, Neveah heard a bark. Then another, then all the dogs were up and barking, snarling, throwing themselves at the bathroom door.

Sarah's voice, over the cacophony: "Are you all right?" Panic infused her words. "Don't open the window."

She thought about opening it just to spite the old bitch. Instead, she opened the door. Dogs poured in around her legs, barely able to stop as they hit the wall under the window. They reared up on hind legs, barking, snarling, hackles raised.

Neveah ran to Sarah, wrapped her arms around her. Buried her head in the great expanse of tits. "Something outside. It knows my name."

Dean on his way. How would he find her here? He wouldn't, that was how. She didn't have anything to worry about. This cabin was tucked away safe.

Sarah stroked her hair. "It's all right. They can't get inside."

"Are you sure?"

She felt Sarah's nod. "They haven't yet."

"Who are they? How do they know who I am?"

"The dogs keep them away. They don't like animals, and animals don't like them. Even if they got in here, the dogs would have them."

Sarah led her to the couch, and they curled together. Neveah could feel Sarah's need, and it embarrassed her. Almost made her pull away, but she couldn't. It wasn't a sexual desire, that Neveah could have handled. This was an emotional pull, a longing to be close to someone. Pathetic, Neveah thought. But she understood it too, somewhere down in the pit of her. She pushed that bullshit away, and teased Sarah, rubbing her back.

The dogs seemed to calm down. They didn't leave the bathroom, but the barking waned to growling, and the growling to snuffling, then silence.

"I'm sorry about earlier."

Sarah stiffened, and she pulled away.

"I just thought... I'm sorry. For some dumb reason I thought you wanted it."

The color drained from Sarah's face and she opened and closed her mouth a few times. "I have a daughter a little younger than you."

"I'm older than I look."

"You're not that old."

"I'm nineteen!"

Sarah laughed. Nineteen. It seemed a lifetime ago. She remembered herself at nineteen, with the girl she used to see back then. Mo, short for Maureen, was her last fling before she met Deborah, Cassie's other mother. Last she'd heard, Mo'd married a banker, and had four children.

"Age is just a number," Neveah said.

Sure it was, until you were the older woman, confronted with a nymph like this one. She might be legal, but that wasn't the only thing that mattered.

"Tell me about yourself," Sarah said. "Are you in college?"

Neveah laughed, and Sarah knew the girl had never set foot in a college classroom. "No one in my family's ever gone to school."

"You could be the first."

She laughed again.

"I used to teach at the University of Vermont," Sarah said.

"No offense, but I want to get out of Vermont, and I want to never, ever come back. I haven't really had a good stay here."

Sarah reminded herself that the girl was a meth addict. She wasn't an upstanding citizen by any means. Sarah didn't need to be involved with anyone.

Yeah. That had been easy to tell herself when she'd been up here alone. Now that she had another person's company, it wasn't quite so simple. *What could it hurt?* she asked herself. For whatever reason, the girl seemed interested. A quick romp, then take her on her way. No one would ever have to know, and maybe for a few hours she could forget the nightmares outside her windows.

Glass broke on the far side of the house, in the kitchen. The window over the sink. The dogs tripped over one another spurting from the bathroom, surging to the kitchen in a sea of fur, all tans, browns, blacks and whites. They sprang up, the black and white bitch getting herself fully up in the sink, throwing herself at the window.

The shutters came open and a hand reached in.

The dog lunged for it, white lips curled back to reveal sharp, yellowed teeth. Sarah knew dogs. As a rule, they didn't like violence. They'd rather avoid conflict. They wanted a warm place to curl up, someone to rub their bellies. Something about *them* drove the dogs to savagery.

The black and white dog's teeth made contact, and red blood spattered the stainless steel. Once she might have expected a cry from whoever had been bitten, but now she knew better. Humans in their thrall stayed silent.

She raised her shotgun, shoved through the dogs, and made her way to the window. One of the brown dogs snapped at her as she passed, he was so agitated. She kicked at him with her foot, not hard, just enough to put him off balance and send him a step away. She forced the muzzle of the gun through the opening between the shutters, pointed down at the ground and fired. One barrel, then the next.

The black and white dog jumped away like she'd been burned, and sat on the kitchen floor, shaking her head. The gun had gone off right near her ears. Sarah's ears rang too, and for a blissful moment she couldn't hear any of the barking or panting around her.

The dogs rushed to the door, and Sarah took the moment to nail three boards across the broken window, the open shutters. She knew she should do all the windows, just board them up. They weren't any good to her anyway. This was taking it too far, though. An admission that it wouldn't end soon, that things weren't going back to normal.

Her hearing came back, slowly, but with a ringing stuck in her right ear. A small price to pay. The dog kept shaking her head, the discomfort pulling her out of the joy of barking at the door.

Sarah's heart pounded in her chest.

Someone got a hand into her home. A man's hand, from the look of it. And her dog had given him a run for his money, even if Sarah's shots hadn't struck home. It was buckshot, so hopefully something hit the mark.

They'd never gotten into her home before. Not since the afternoon Cavender came to pay a visit, when she'd quickly realized he wasn't quite right. They'd gotten to him. It made her shudder.

"Did you shoot him?" Neveah sat curled on the couch, in the smallest ball she could arrange herself in. She'd maneuvered herself so her back wasn't to any of the windows.

"I don't know."

"Who was he? Is he who you're afraid of?"

"Him and others."

"Why do they want to hurt you?"

How much to tell her? She was here, cowering and afraid in the middle of the night, so he supposed she deserved something. "I know too much about them."

"Are they, like, the mob or something? Drug dealers?"

She seemed to perk up at the idea of drug dealers, as though they were something she knew about, had experience with. Context.

Sarah shook her head.

"Will they come back?" Neveah's voice was small, like a little girl's. Her eyes were big and brown. After the shower all traces of her dark make-up were gone. She looked older without it. More mature, anyway. Not as much like she was playing dress up with mommy's eye shadow. Sarah wanted to comfort her, but was afraid to. Neveah was a sexual creature, and Sarah didn't know what to make of that. So she checked all the other shutters, taking a moment to catch her breath when she was alone in the bedroom and the bathroom.

Against her better judgment, Sarah sat down on the futon next to Neveah. The girl wrapped her arms around her, drawing her close. The poor thing was shaking. "Will they come back?"

Sarah waffled between telling her the truth and sugar coating things. She decided on the former. "I'm not sure they ever leave."

They sat in solemn silence for a few beats. "Who are they?" she asked again. "I think I should know. I'm, like, here too."

"You'll be gone tomorrow."

Neveah snuggled in closer. Sarah's warning bells blared, but Neveah's warmth felt good to her. She'd gone so long with no contact with anyone but the dogs. Dogs she refused to even name.

In the secret, darkest part of her mind she'd started referring to the spotted bitch as "Freckles." It was a dumb name, but something about her was a Freckles.

Maybe it wouldn't hurt to let someone else in. Common sense suggested she ought to start with the dogs, but Neveah shifted beside her, around her, and they were kissing again. Sarah let her mind go, floating to the past, to old lovers, to fantasies she would never dare share with anyone. Neveah was a good kisser. Practiced.

After a few moments, the girl pulled away. "Is this okay?" she asked.

Sort of the equivalent of shooting first, asking questions later. Sarah, breathless, nodded. Neveah kissed her again. She ran her hands up and down Sarah's arms, outside her flannel sleeves. Suddenly, it was very hot in the cabin, the woodstove throwing an awful lot of heat out into the little space. Neveah touched her hair, brushing it out of her face.

She was afraid to move. Afraid that if she did, she wouldn't be able to stop herself. Now Neveah kissed her neck, leaving her to gasp for air.

"No more."

"You said it was okay."

"I know. But I can't. I can't do this." Sarah grasped for some reason, something to use as a weapon. "No. You're a drug addict."

"What does that have to do with anything?" Twin patches of red sprang up on Neveah's cheeks. "What bullshit is that? So I like to have a little fun. What the fuck does that have to do with anything?" She scooted back on the futon, then stood. "I'm the best piece of ass you're likely to ever get, and you throw it away? For what? Your survivalist bullshit in a cabin in the woods with dogs who don't even have names? Who the fuck is out there?"

It had been a long time since Sarah had seen such anger. Neveah stormed, smashed a lamp to the floor. It didn't matter, it wasn't on, but its ceramic base shattered. Such pain. She felt bad for it, deeply bad. But she didn't want to open herself to...

To whatever it was that Neveah had to offer.

You can't trust drug addicts.

"Since you won't fucking tell me, I'm going to look for myself."

A moment ago, she'd been watching Neveah rage, letting her get out her anger. Again she reminded Sarah of Mo, whose fury had also flashed hot and melted away quickly. Now panic clamped down on her spine, and instead of feeling hot she was cold, the sweat she'd worked up turning to ice on her skin.

"No." Sarah stood.

Neveah dodged around her, lithe and quick. Sarah reached out and snatched some of her tank top. When the girl twisted, Sarah again saw those awful bruises on her ribs and stomach. Neveah tugged free, and marched to the door.

"No!" Sarah screamed to her. *She couldn't.*

The dogs swirled, agitated. Three of them surged for the door with Neveah.

Freckles and a tan male hung back with Sarah, uncertain, and she had to push them aside. In that wasted time, Neveah threw open the cabin's door.

10 – SOMETHING FROM THE SEA

Fuck the bitch. Neveah did her a fucking favor—kissing her neck, whatever. Then the bitch told her to get off because she was too dirty? Because she was a tramp? Fuck her. How nice for her that she didn't have to fuck anyone to get paid. What a fucking luxury.

She stormed towards the door, her tears coming unbidden. What did she care? Why the fuck was she crying? The old bitch did her a favor, stopping her. She shoved a dog aside with her foot and opened the door.

Outside, the night was silent and cool. Moonlight played through bare branches, and LED security lights brightened the side of the garage in a freaky blue light.

Nothing fucking out here. Big goddamned surprise. Fuck, she wanted to get out of here so bad. Who cared if she were safe from Dean here? Hell, the voices said she wasn't.

She wheeled on the woman as four dogs forced past her and out into the night.

"There's nothing fucking out here, you lying, paranoid bitch."

Sarah looked past her, her mouth dropping to a flat line, lips pressing tight, forcing the blood away. She held the black and white dog by the collar, and it fought to get away, fought to get out into the night.

"Get back in here." The quiet and calm in her voice as she battled the dog jolted Neveah out of her tantrum.

It was behind her.

She stood with her back to the woods, to the spidery branches. She could hear the dogs, hear them growling and barking, then they went silent, like they'd found their mark and were analyzing what to do with it. Sarah vanished into the house, and Neveah heard her locking the last dog in the bathroom. She came out with the shotgun.

"Get in the house, Neveah."

First, Neveah had to turn around. Her mouth was dry and tears streamed down her face—the tears of rage had suddenly became tears of fear.

It wasn't a person behind her.

She wasn't sure how she knew this—knew it was a thing and not a human—but she did. Sarah screamed at her, "Get in the goddamn house!" Neveah ran. With each step she imagined it behind her, imagined it reaching out with claw-like fingers. The footprints she'd seen, the claw marks—this had to be them. She imagined claws in her hair and when she got to Sarah she clung to her, moved behind her. Only then did she look.

She was met with the yelp of one of the dogs, the tan male she liked so much. He flew back, hitting the ground, not moving.

You did this. You hurt—killed?—the dog. You let him out. You did this.

Thinking about the dog, blaming herself, meant she didn't have to think about the thing that threw the dog on the ground.

If it had wings, why did it walk, and not fly?

How did it see? Instead of a face it had... Polyps? She wasn't sure that was the right word, but it reminded her of a thing she'd seen at an aquarium once, with reaching stubby tentacle things, all white like it had never seen the sun or daylight.

The legs. There were so many of them. It stood on four, another four reaching for the dogs.

Neveah's ears went dead as Sarah shot the thing with both barrels.

The woman appeared to say something to her, but she couldn't hear it. Sarah's mouth moved, and her eyebrows curved down in an unhappy line.

The insectile voice she'd heard before was back, screaming as part of the segmented torso burst apart. Was that called a thorax? Another word from the aquarium trip that maybe wasn't right. The thing raised two pairs of arms and waggled them at the sky, furious at being shot. The wings beat, sluggish and feeble, and then it dropped to its... knees? Did it have knees?

The screaming went on and on, and Sarah dropped her shells as she struggled to reload. Neveah worried the woman would drop the shotgun, her hands were shaking so hard, but she leveled it, took a steadying breath, and shot again.

This time a dog yelped, and Sarah started to sob, but the thing's keening cut off sharply. It landed face first on the cut grass between the driveway and the house. The woman started towards it. The dogs kept a wary distance, but were growing bolder as it didn't move. Neveah, still clutching her, followed.

"Either get in the goddamn house or help me with the dogs!"

Neveah felt like her mind was moving in slow motion, like an old movie reel gone too slow. One image clunking into place after another.

"Let go of me!" A whine crept into Sarah's voice, a panic, a desperation, and Neveah did. Back in the house or get a dog? Which one? She had to choose. Sarah grabbed the two unhurt dogs by the collar and passed Neveah, dragging them back into the house. They whined and chuffed and squirmed, but it seemed like they too would rather be separated from these things by a wall. They went in the bathroom, with the black and white dog.

Help with the dogs, or go back in the house? Neveah tried to work through the problem like it was math, if x then y. How could she decide? Sarah was back outside, hefting the two hurt dogs, one under each arm, two sacks of grain. One squirmed, swung its head around, bit her arm. It broke the skin and her blood ran down her pale hand, red-black in the harsh light.

"Get in the house!" A note of pleading crept into her voice.

Neveah realized the choice had been made for her. Dogs were done, no longer did Sarah need help with them. So she needed to go in the house.

Her legs were cement until, in the corner of the garage, she saw another of the things, and a man.

"Sarah!" she shrieked, and pointed. Sarah slung the dogs into the house. One got to its feet and scurried away, clearly pissed off. The other slumped there in a furry heap.

There was a reason the woman didn't name the dogs.

Sarah fired her shotgun a third time, and the ringing sensation in Neveah's ears was somehow finally enough to make her feet move. She ran for the house, shoving the hurt dog—the one who'd bitten Sarah—back inside.

Sarah followed, throwing the bar to lock the door. She dropped to the floor, wrapped her hands around her knees, and took deep sucking breaths.

"What are they?" Neveah asked. The back of her throat tasted like snot and she was pretty sure she was yelling because with the ringing in her ears, she couldn't tell how loud she was being.

Sarah ignored her, maybe hadn't heard her. Maybe her ears were fucked up too, so Neveah moved around where Sarah could see her, and asked again.

The vacant look left Sarah's eyes, and she glared at Neveah.

Neveah hadn't had an easy life. Her mother and step dad were assholes to her, her older sister was awful, her first pimp was a shit, and Dean was pretty rotten. She didn't think anyone had ever glared at her with the enmity contained in Sarah's eyes.

"Get out of my sight. You did this to my dogs."

She pushed herself up, pushed past Neveah, and went to the fallen dog. This was the one who'd been attacked by the thing, who wasn't moving. Neveah faltered. Sarah was right, of course, but it wasn't like she'd done it simply to be cruel. She'd been in pain. Sarah'd turned her down. Called her dirty. A whore.

Rage waggled in her again.

She went to the other dog instead, the one who'd been hit with the buckshot and bit Sarah. It bared its teeth at her, so she backed off, standing awkwardly.

Sarah put her face on the dog's chest, listening for a heartbeat. She jerked her head up, and rushed into the bathroom. She came back with a bottle of hydrogen peroxide, and poured it down the unconscious dog's throat.

The dog came to, brown eyes opening to slits. Its body heaved as it threw up the peroxide in a foamy mass. Within the white of the foam were whorls of sickish green. The puke stank, and Neveah covered her mouth.

They were still tending to the dogs when dawn broke. Sarah had yelled at her, sure, but through sheer persistence, Neveah'd gotten back in her good graces. "Can I open the door?" She asked.

Sarah grunted assent. Neveah did, and the three healthy dogs scurried out to do their business. The wounded dog, seemingly not too worse for the wear, limped outside to join the others. Neveah went out into the grey dawn. The sky above was the color of pewter, pink to the east, navy to the west. The morning was almost completely silent, other than the sounds the dogs made. Far off, she could hear the stream on the rocks.

Neveah didn't know nature, but this was the first time she'd noticed there weren't any birds.

What she really wanted to see lay dead in the grass. It was pink, the exact color between the pewter and the rose of the sky, a sickly, pallid hue. She wondered what it looked like alive, in the light. She scanned the woodline, but realized that the dogs' placid behavior meant they were safe.

It was ugly, and not as big as it seemed in the darkness. It reminded her of a crab, a wasp, and something from the sea, all in one awful animal. Its wings stretched out behind it on the grass.

"Two of them died in the flooding." Sarah didn't have to specify what flooding. After Irene, there was no question in anyone's mind. Even Neveah, not a Vermonter, had been affected by the nightmare hurricane. "The bodies got caught up in the Winooski River, and washed downstream."

"Other people know about these things?" Neveah asked.

Sarah gave a half shrug.

"Do you have a camera? Take pictures of it!"

Sarah shook her head. "They can't be photographed. Don't show up. And as soon as the sun hits it, it'll turn into a sludge. They can't be preserved."

"What are they?"

"Aliens."

She sounded foolish, saying it out loud, but it's what they were. Aliens. And they wanted her to go with them, past the edges of the solar system, back to their place.

Questions stampeded across Neveah's face. She looked like she didn't want to believe it, but felt compelled to. The proof lay dead at her feet, after all. She finally decided on a question. "Why are they here?"

"There are metals on earth they can't get where they're from."

"How do you know that?"

"They've told me."

Neveah took a step back.

We need your help. Someone like you. Someone to study our folklore, to chronicle it, document it for us. Our culture is changing, and soon no one will remember the old ways. It was supposed to be nice to be needed. But they'd told her how they traveled, and she wasn't willing to make that step.

"Why are they harassing you?"

"I know too much about them. They don't like it when we get too curious."

"What did you do?"

"I think the last straw came when I recorded them—you've heard them, they sound like bugs, buzzing. I recorded it on my phone and sent it to a folklorist down in Massachusetts."

"What did he say?"

"I don't think she believes me. I think she thinks I'm crazy." And why wouldn't she? Sarah's letters—she didn't trust email, and the phone didn't work out here anymore—had grown more and more bizarre over the past few months. She knew how she sounded, she wasn't stupid. She imagined herself, six months ago, receiving letters like the ones she'd sent

Dr. Leary. Except... She'd grown up in these woods. She knew things weren't quite as they seemed or should be. She knew there had always been an "other" type of feeling here. It was part of the reason she hadn't wanted to leave. Like her own private Bigfoot.

Now, every day, she thought more and more about going to be with her daughter. Cassie'd told her to come to California, told her she'd like the climate and the people and the Pacific. Maybe she was right.

She thought of Cassie, then stole a glance at Neveah, a juxtaposition of angles and curves. Sharp elbows and knees, soft hips and breasts.

Sarah looked back at the thing on the ground, disgusted with herself. She'd been under siege almost a month, though. This creature wasn't new or novel any more, it was routine. They came every night, the aliens or their human lackeys. One night Asa Gardner had nearly made it into her house, and she hadn't had her shotgun loaded. She'd managed to hit him with it before he grabbed her and dragged her out, but damn, had he been close. She'd almost been outside with him. And what then?

She had an idea, though she didn't know the mechanics—and she hoped to never know them.

"What are you going to do?"

"Leave," Sarah said, though it came out as more of a question. "I don't *want* to. I've lived here all my life. I grew up here. I don't want to go."

"You said they want to take you when they go?"

Did Neveah think she was crazy? Probably. She nodded.

"Take you where?"

Sarah looked up. "Home. Space. I don't know where they're from exactly."

Neveah chewed her lip and rolled a lock of hair around on her fingers. "Now that it's daytime, they can't get to us, right? So we're safe until dark?"

"They have human agents. Those can get to us any time. But the things don't do well in the sunlight. Look." Sarah pointed outside, and Neveah went to the window. The corpse looked deflated and sunken. "It'll be gone within the hour."

"So no pictures and no body. No one would ever believe you."

The dogs pricked up their ears and went to the door. With a sad pit in her stomach, Sarah knew that once the road was cleared, she ought to pack up and go. Stop fighting, stop everything, and head for California.

Every time she came to this realization though, she'd look around. Her home. The house and the land were paid for, no outstanding mortgage. The car was paid for too. It was more than that, though. The way the little plot of earth sat tucked in among the mountains, the way the sun hit at dusk and dawn. The pleasure of watching deer in the meadow—back when there were deer here. It wasn't right they should take this from her.

"What's that?" Neveah went to the door with the dogs, peering out.

Where the alien once lay, a thick puddle slicked the grass. Soon even that would be gone. Sarah shook her head. "I don't hear anything."

"Machinery. I think they're clearing the road."

Funny. She would have expected the girl to sound more excited. "Let's go look."

"Why? They're just moving some trees." Neveah stared down at her boots. "They're going to get it done whether we're out there or not."

"I thought you wanted to get to Boston."

Neveah raised her brown eyes, and met Sarah's gaze. She looked away, bashful. "Yeah."

Something in Sarah flexed. Was she having second thoughts about going? A herd of thoughts stampeded through her mind. *She* was leaving. Neveah was a teenage addict. She was pretty, but she knew other women who'd become involved with younger partners, and it never managed to end well.

Sarah headed outside. She left the dogs behind. They'd bark and make a nuisance of themselves. She wanted to see the work progressing, wanted to feel something normal was going on. Road crews fixing a problem, getting a paycheck. How long had it been since Sarah had done that? She pushed the thought from her mind. It had nothing to do with aliens or intruders.

Neveah popped up beside her, quiet as a little mouse. She'd pulled one of Sarah's flannel shirts on over her tank top, and it dwarfed her. She wrapped it around herself. Now that the heavy eyeliner was gone, she looked more like the kind of woman Sarah wanted to be with. She tried to carry herself with confidence, but just didn't have it. Underneath faux bravado, the girl slunk around like a whipped dog.

Sarah reached for her hand, and took it.

"Tell me about your name," Sarah said, to pass the time. They spoke in a hush, and the happy stream sounds danced around them.

Neveah gave an embarrassed smile. "It's like heaven, backwards. But my Mom didn't like the spelling that way. So she changed it. So I'm like almost heaven."

Sarah smiled too, and let herself feel almost normal in that moment. Two women out for a walk, sharing each other's company. Nothing sinister, nothing hinkey. Just two friends. Together.

Neveah's fingers wound around her own. "I'm sorry I got upset," she said. "I didn't realize—I didn't get it. I didn't know how serious things were. I thought—I don't know what I thought. It wasn't this, though. I'm so sorry."

Sarah squeezed her hand. "I should have been more honest with you. I didn't think you'd believe me."

"It's crazy, you know? I've never seen anything like those things. They're so scary."

They'd go once the road was clear. Both of them. First to Boston, where she could hand-deliver Neveah wherever she needed to go. She didn't want to think about the girl out there alone, hitchhiking again. What if someone else had picked her up? Sarah shuddered.

The sounds of chainsaws and the rumbling diesel engine grew louder. They could hear men calling to one another, a woman's voice interspersed. Sarah caught glimpses. There was Asa Gardner, Christina Marlowe, Ken Abbott—who Sarah was fairly sure knew nothing about the malice that shrouded them—and another man, one she didn't recognize.

Neveah froze. "Let's go back."

"They've almost got the westbound tree out. They'll start on the eastbound one soon."

"No, they won't." Her voice was reduced to a breathy whisper, her color pale. "They're cutting that tree so they can get in to us, not so we can get out. Let's go back. When they come, you have to hide me."

The girl turned back to the cabin. Sarah followed. Neveah's long dark ponytail swayed with the same rhythm as her hips as she retreated to the house. It had to be the man she didn't recognize. He had to be someone to Neveah.

"Who was he?" Sarah asked. "Who was the guy?"

Neveah shook her head.

"Maybe I can help."

"He's the reason I want to go to Boston."

"Is he a boyfriend?" Sarah hated herself for what the word did to her. So Neveah liked both. That was all right. A flare of anger sparked in herself—she had to stop thinking like this. The girl was too young, her anger was too much. They weren't anything to each other. Just two people trapped in a circumstance. If they ran into each other on the street in Brattleboro, they wouldn't have even exchanged the time.

Neveah half nodded. She stopped, turned, and fixed her gaze on Sarah. Intense eye contact. "He's going to kill me."

12 – HIDING

Neveah had expected to find more monsters, or townspeople in the aliens' throes. She hadn't expected Dean. Seeing his hunched shoulders and his bright purple jacket made her stomach feel like she might puke. He'd followed her here. How had he known? She'd hitched with two different guys, come east through Podunk towns as opposed to heading straight south back to New York. There was no reason to think she'd come this way... Unless the guy who took her bag with the drugs went back to Dean to tell him? But how would the asshole have known whose junk she was carrying?

"This is really bad." She didn't let her voice go too loud. She walked quickly, pushing them back to the house. The cabin sat tucked in a little clearing, hemmed in by steep mountains. This was essentially a dead end. She was wearing an old pair of Chuck Taylor sneakers. She wouldn't get far in the mountains, even assuming she managed to evade the alien things.

She was well and truly fucked.

"Do you have a place where you can hide me if he comes?"

Sarah thought for a moment. She did everything so slowly and deliberately, it made Neveah want to scream. She couldn't wait to get out of here—but where would she go? Maybe Dean would come, look around, not find her, and go about his business. Sarah could say she'd gone to Boston before the big tree fell. Could say she'd never even seen her.

"There's hay up in the loft in the barn."

Hay... and spiders, and fuck knew what else. Ick. It would have to do.

"Tell me about him?" Sarah said.

Neveah thought about it. If Sarah'd resisted her

advances because she was a junkie, she'd be safe from anything in the future if she told the whole story.

"He's not my boyfriend," she said, letting the words lie dramatically. "I mean, he kind of is." Unbidden, she recalled the rare night where she and Dean just hung out. Pizza, a movie, fooling around without anyone getting paid. She hated herself for liking those nights. Reminded herself he was a master manipulator, which was why he was so good at what he did. Reminded herself he had nights like that with Sierra and with Evvie, too. But he made her feel so special. He made her laugh.

"He deals drugs." She took a deep breath. Made it really look like she was struggling with inner demons. "And he's my pimp."

Sarah brought a hand to her mouth.

Neveah started to cry. "You were right not to fuck me." She stuttered her words with her sobs. "I'm dirty and broken. No one's ever loved me." As expected, Sarah scooped her up in her arms, running fingers through her hair and whispering it was all right, she was safe now, they'd get out of here together.

"I'll get you to Boston, I promise."

Neveah pulled away, wiping at her nose and her eyes. "That's not all."

Drugs and whores clearly weren't a part of Sarah's college-educated, rural Vermont life. She nodded, encouraging Neveah to go on, trying to be supportive.

"I stole drugs from him. I thought it would help me get away. Like I could sell them on my way." This part stung. It hurt, and made her feel stupid. Weak. Less than herself. "The second guy who picked me up..."

The first guy had been happy to give her a ride and anything she wanted at McDonalds for a blowjob. He'd been cute and clean and he was legit nice to her before and after. Neveah'd been on top of the world—between the drugs and her body, she was in a power seller position. The second guy drove an old truck, and she'd started by offering the drugs, not sex. The ultimate goal was to not have to rent parts of her body by the hour, and she was riding high after how kind the first guy'd been. So she said she'd give him a quarter gram for a ride as far west as he was headed.

His eyes lit up, and she got a good feeling about it. She'd be in Boston later that day, she'd figured. She could smoke up, relax, and figure out what next.

So she got in the car.

He hadn't been as nice as the other guy. He'd figured, correctly, she wasn't about to hand over all the junk she had, and that her backpack contained more than just a dime bag. He'd helped himself. Punched her a few times when she'd tried to fight, hitting her in some of the same places Dean did, nailing her in the rib she thought might be broken. Taken the drugs, dropped her ass off in some shit heap called Wickenden. He'd left her on the side of the road by some river, at a nice little turn off with picnic tables and a spot to view the water rushing over smooth rocks. He told her she could have a dime bag if she showed him her tits, but by then she was so upset she got out of the car, relinquishing her backpack.

Now she thought maybe she should have done it. A hit would be awesome. Might shove the memory of that *thing* out there from her mind. Might help her forget she was a dirty whore, and that fucking *Dean* was here looking for his drugs.

Sarah watched her, waiting for the rest of the story.

"He took the drugs, took my wallet, took everything I had. I was going to use the meth to pay my way, get myself settled... Now I have nothing."

"Do you have a place to go in Boston?"

She half nodded. She was pretty sure Tito would let her crash. She'd been 100% sure when it had been her and a backpack of crystal.

Sarah frowned at her.

***

Neveah chewed over what Sarah had told her earlier. "They want to take you to space?"

Sarah took a deep breath and settled herself on the futon, drawing a blanket across her lap. Neveah chose to stand. She leaned against the cool woodstove, where she could see down the driveway. She didn't know what she would do if she suddenly saw Dean through the window.

"They won't take our bodies."

The word *our* and the pluralization of *bodies* made Neveah shiver, and run her hands down her sides a little from where her arms were crossed. She wanted to feel herself, a reminder she was still there.

"It's easier for them to just take our minds. They extract our essence, our consciousness, what makes us *us,* and that's what they take with them when they go." Neveah got it that the *us* Sarah talked about wasn't specific to the two of them, but to humankind. "They took my neighbor. The guy out there with the chainsaw. His wife. She was a scientist, super smart. I bet she was excited to be taken. Seems like something she'd really have wanted. Would want." Sarah let a beat pass before she continued. "He buried her body under the wood pile."

"How do you know her consciousness got out? How do you know he didn't just kill her?"

"I guess I don't. They could be lying to me. But if they wanted to kill me, they could."

Outside, the sounds of the chainsaws stopped.

"I should hide," Neveah said.

Sarah stood, folded the blanket, and walked Neveah out to the barn. The big door ran on a slider, and it made miserable creaking, groaning sounds when Sarah hefted it open. She gestured for Neveah to go first up a rickety ladder, and fretted about both of their weight on the wooden rungs. Neveah went up, getting a splinter in her finger.

Sarah followed. "Make a little nest for yourself in there. You'll hear the door if anyone comes in. I'll be sure the other door is locked from inside."

"Where's the other door?" She could see the big one from up here.

"Underneath us."

"Is it loud?"

"No. But I'll lock it, so you won't have to worry about it."

"Are there, like, rats and stuff in here?"

"Don't worry about it. Nothing in here will bother you unless you bother it."

What was that supposed to mean? "Where do those things live when they're hiding for the day?" The sweet-smelling hay didn't feel like a haven any more. If she could hide in it, who knew what else could? Better to hide in the hay than deal with Dean, though. She thought of him, thought of his fists. The things he made her do. She snuggled into the hay, doing as Sarah suggested. She put herself in a little canyon, with big walls looming to the sides, easily swept over her.

"Stay away from the windows."

"I'm not stupid."

"I'll try and talk loud if he comes—they may clear the road and keep going."

"He's here looking for me. He'll come to ask. He wants his property back."

"If you tell him it's gone—" Sarah kept talking, but Neveah didn't hear it. *Tell him the drugs were gone? He'd kill her.*

"I'm not talking about his drugs, I'm talking about me."

That shut her up. Hopefully made her feel bad about calling her a slut and a whore earlier.

Sarah backed up a few steps. "Be safe."

Neveah turned away. She studied each individual bit of hay until she heard Sarah retreat down the ladder. There was a shuffle and a clunk beneath her—Sarah locking the door?—then a squealing grind of the big door opening and closing.

Then she waited, wondering what it might be like to send her consciousness to space.

13 – IN A HEARTBEAT

Sarah didn't have to wait long for Dean to arrive. She let the three dogs out and they milled around the brownish grass left behind where the thing had vanished. They looked around, searching for an enemy, but the enemy was gone. Sarah made tea and sat out on her porch, something she hadn't done for months. She willed her hands not to shake, and forced herself not to steal glances up at the barn windows.

Soon, the dogs started barking, and rushed down the driveway. Along came Dean, walking with Asa Gardner.

She didn't like the looks of him from the get-go. He seemed like a thug, and the closer he got, the more he confirmed her opinion. His swagger, oversized pants, big puffy jacket, and ball cap with a flat, straight brim, it all screamed attitude.

"Hi, Sarah. How are you this afternoon?" Asa called. She thought of the shotgun just inside the doorway, and wondered what would happen if she used it on them. Plenty of space out here to hide a body.

"You boys get the trees cleared out on the road?"

"Oh, no, not yet. Just the one on the downhill side. Going to be a while before we can get to the other."

"And why's that?"

"I've got errands to run, got to get in to work tomorrow." Asa wasn't a good liar.

"Why aren't the town crews out here working?"

"Was a big storm, lots of trees down. This one's not the highest priority."

Of course it wasn't. She and Neveah weren't trapped up here any more, but they couldn't get out without going through Wickenden, where lots of prying eyes waited. The trio lingered in silence, Sarah sitting in her chair, the men hovering awkwardly. The dogs watched from the grass.

"I heard you picked up a hitchhiker," Dean said.

They had eyes everywhere. They saw everything.

"Picked her up a little east of town. Couldn't give her much of a ride, but dropped her out there on the road. She's likely halfway to Bellows Falls by now."

Dean's eyes, shadowed by his hat, narrowed. "She's my girlfriend. I'm worried about her. I want to make sure she gets home safe." He sounded sincere, but Sarah knew he wasn't.

"She didn't say anything about a boyfriend. Said she was trying to get to New York City. I told her it was the wrong way for the city, and she said she needed to make a stop in Keene first."

"New York?" Dean echoed her, his tone bleak. He didn't believe her. Not one bit. "Not Boston?"

"Nope. Definitely New York. I told her she was headed in the wrong direction. I didn't even get her name."

Dean ignored the last. "Mind if I look around?"

"You think after two days she's still here?"

"She could be. I don't know what you two talked about on your ride, but she's little better than a sociopath. She'll say anything, do anything, to get what she wants. One minute she has you thinking she's your best friend, the next she's all claws and poison."

His words hit her as true, and Sarah felt the spit drain from her mouth. He was abusive, she reminded herself. A manipulator. Of course he would say those things. *What would a pretty young girl want with someone like her?*

"She has something of mine, and I want it back."

"She didn't have anything. No bags. Not even a jacket."

Dean's face went dark again, the corners of his plump lips turning down. "Nothing?"

"She said she was robbed by the last guy she hitched from."

Dean kept his face flat, but his Adam's apple bobbed up and down. "She wasn't carrying anything?"

"I told you, no."

Dean pounced on her. Over his shoulder, she caught sight of Asa's mouth forming a surprised "O". He reached forward tentatively, as if to haul Dean off. Then he pulled his hand back, and retreated a step. Sarah's head hit the porch with a loud crack and her vision jumped. Pulsing waves of pain radiated from the spot she'd hit. She felt sick to her stomach, like she might puke.

"Where's the backpack?" Dean was up in her face, and the minty scent of his breath overwhelmed all the other smells in her world. He was very well groomed, she couldn't help but notice. Neatly shaven, eyebrows plucked or waxed into a pleasing shape.

"She never had a backpack." It came out a whisper, and it embarrassed her. She was taller and bigger than Dean, but he was a solid, scrappy little guy, and she had no doubt that he could overpower her. The presence of his body on top of hers made her skin crawl. She wanted him off, away, out of her space.

"I'm going to look around."

Sarah nodded, fresh waves of pain radiating from her head. Dean shoved her back down onto the porch, and stood up. She caught sight of white boxers with red dots. She didn't want to know what his underwear looked like. It was invasive and awful.

The dogs stood by, heads down, tails up, evaluating.

Maybe if she'd named them, they would have fought for her. The thought drew tears to her eyes.

Dean showed himself into the house, and she heard the sounds of his search—smashings and overturnings. Violence done to her things.

It didn't matter, she was leaving tonight anyway. What would they think when they found her gone, her home ransacked? Would anyone notice? Would they care? Would the police come?

She hauled herself up into a sitting position and fixed her glare on Asa, who looked everywhere he could think of that wasn't her.

"Are you happy?" she asked.

He cast a sad smile her way. Like he pitied her. "Just give in. Go with them."

"Why don't you?"

He shook his shaggy head. "They don't want just *anyone*. They don't want me. But you... I know they want you. It's an honor. If I could go in your place I would, in a heartbeat."

"If it were up to me, you could have my spot."

"I appreciate that, Sarah."

Dean appeared in the doorway. It hurt Sarah's head to crane around to see him. "I don't see it."

"Because it's not there. She left. She never even came to my house."

"No? Who've you got visiting then? Who'd you have lunch with? Or are you such a fat cow that you're eating for two?"

Sarah struggled to her feet, and took a step towards him. He shoved her and she fell hard, half on the porch, half on the grass below. The black and white dog, *Freckles*, took a step forward, growling.

"Call that mangy-ass thing off before I shoot it. Let me look in your barn."

"Like I could stop you," she said, reaching for Freckles' collar, holding her back.

Dean liked the sound of that. "Now you get it." He nodded, walking past, bringing his sneaker down deadly close to her fingers. She yanked her hand back and placed it on the dog's collar, holding on with both hands. She felt the growl down low in the dog's throat.

Outside Asa and Dean's gaze, she let her fingers slide crossed, willing them not to find Neveah. She knew she could get her shotgun, but violence would beget violence. If she escalated things by producing a firearm, they would retaliate. Dean must be carrying a gun.

Neveah would have the sense to cover herself and stay quiet.

Sarah heard them trying the back door, struggling to get it open. "The front's unlocked!" she shouted. They went around the far side of the barn, and she heard the grinding of the door peeling open. She stood, wobbling on her feet, and headed to watch. She still held Freckles' collar. The other two dogs followed at a distance. The tan male she named Loki, and the black one Anansi. They seemed to be tricksters, and to have senses of humor.

It was easier to name her dogs than to think about what would happen if Dean found Neveah. She'd have to hide in the back, under cover, in the car on the way through Wickenden.

Asa sauntered out of the barn.

"You don't look so good."

"Why are you helping him?"

"His gal's gone missing. They told us you have her."

"I don't have her. I would have run from someone like him, too."

"He's a man who knows what he wants."

Dean started to climb the ladder. Sarah turned away, scanning the forested edges of her property. She couldn't look. She willed herself to stop clenching her fists.

Maybe she couldn't look, but she couldn't look away. She spun herself back around and watched as he got to the top of the wooden ladder. That poor thing had seen more traffic today than in the half-decade preceding it. She willed it to give way under his weight.

The rungs groaned, but held. He stepped into the hayloft.

Sarah distracted herself by wondering what Cassie would do when she showed up on her doorstep.

A second thought crowded in. What would Cassie think if she showed up on her doorstep with a girl a year younger than she was? Cassie would tell Deborah, and Sarah would get a call from her, full of faux concern. Fuck you, Deborah, with your perfect wife and house and life. It made her sick as Dean picked his way around the edges of the hayloft.

He didn't spend long up there. Neveah must be good at staying still, because he started back towards the ladder.

If Sarah had been focusing on him instead of floating in her head, she would have seen it sooner. Dean was afraid of heights.

The ladder groaned a bit more as he made his way down, and now that she knew what to look for, she could see how tight he clung to each rung, and how gingerly he moved his feet. When he stepped back onto terra firma he took a half second to compose himself—she might have missed it if she didn't recognize the signs. He stormed up to her.

"Where is she?"

"I told you, I dropped her—"

Dean slapped her. It wasn't a hard slap, but in partnership with her aching head, bells rang and she saw stars. She'd always thought it was an expression, nothing more, but she actually saw bright flashes of white in her field of vision.

Asa caught Freckles by the collar as she lunged. The dog spun, snapping at his wrist, catching his skin with her teeth. He let go, and Sarah caught her. She didn't bite, but whined, wanting to be released.

"I'm going to wait here. She's hiding somewhere. The woods, maybe? I'm going to wait right here, until she comes out."

"She's not here."

"You're going to quit your fucking lying to me."

They all went inside. Sarah closed the door behind them with a gentle click.

14 – LIKE ALL THE GOOD PARTS OF DEATH WITHOUT ANY OF THE BAD

Neveah imagined she was dead. Imagined the hay poking her nose, her knees, imagined her bruised rib didn't exist. She was dead, she was meat, she was a thing. Nothing mattered, except being silent.

She'd actually stopped breathing when she heard him come up the ladder.

She hadn't thought he'd do it. Thought he'd chicken out, maybe send Sarah or the other man up. But he'd come.

When she left, she'd said she'd never see him again. She still hadn't, but it was too close for comfort. Only when she heard him back on the ladder had she dared breathe again. She matched her exhalations to his ragged ones.

Then he was gone.

She heard them talking in the barn, heard the dogs bark a bit, then nothing. She had to pee. It crossed her mind to just do it here where she lay, but instead she started to uncover herself, let the cool air in, get rid of some of the poking hay bits.

The aliens wanted to take Sarah to space.

Dean would never look for Neveah in space. She'd be left alone from all the assholes who wanted to use her. Without her body, she wouldn't be exploited. So how to get them to take her?

She stood and walked to over to the window. She made sure to position herself off to one side, so if they happened to look up they wouldn't see her. The yard and driveway seemed empty. She tugged down her shorts and pissed in the corner of the loft. There were aliens. Sarah had worse problems than some pee in her barn.

When she finished, waggling to drip dry, she went back to the window. No sign of motion. Sarah planned to get them out of here, but Neveah couldn't let that happen. This was where they were the safest, where Neveah had the best chance of being taken by Sarah's visitors.

She headed down the ladder. The wood creaked under her weight, so she moved as quickly as she could down to the barn floor below. Four summer tires sat piled on the concrete floor. She'd thought she would take the distributor cap from Sarah's Subaru, but she'd realized she didn't actually know what a distributor cap was, where to find it, or how to remove it. Slashing the tires would have to do. She didn't know how it would work, exactly, didn't know how easily these other tires could be put on the car, so she found a screwdriver and set to work stabbing and slashing at the black rubber. When she finished, she slipped the screwdriver into the pocket of her skinny jeans. It stuck up and out of the pocket, almost to her ribs.

She went to the locked back door and twisted the knob. From inside, it popped open, and swung towards her on silent hinges. Slipping out into the afternoon, she eased it shut and hurried to the far side of the barn, away from the windows of the house. It was eerie how quiet it was out here. No birds, no bugs. She didn't spend a lot of time outside, but she knew enough to be freaked out a little by the silence. Animals didn't like the aliens. The aliens would deliver her from Dean. It was a good thing.

She sprinted through the open area and ducked behind the car, where she went to work on the first tire. The Subaru sagged towards her as the tires lost air. Good.

She had started on the second when she heard something, an animal sound. Against the quiet, it made the little hairs stand up on the back of her neck, and she worked the screwdriver free from the tire and held it up.

A dog. Fuck. One of the dogs was out. That meant—
Fuck!

Strong arms grabbed her from behind, wrapped around her middle. Pressure on her bruises, her broken ribs. She screamed. But she didn't let the pain stop her. Wheeling with the screwdriver, she stabbed back, striking something soft, digging in.

There was a hiss of breath.

She didn't need to look to know it was Dean. She could smell his cologne, his deodorant, the unmistakable "Dean" smell underneath all that. She felt the squish of the purple FUBU jacket he loved.

With his free hand he grabbed hers, the one holding the screwdriver, and squeezed. Her bones ground together and she let out a little hissing gasp before letting go. The screwdriver clattered to the ground, and he picked her up easily.

His voice, in her ear. "You think you can get away from me?"

She kicked and spat, tried to claw at him, but he had her. Every time she moved, her broken rib howled, and the pain made her woozy. She didn't have time for woozy. His arms were strong, arms that had hit her and had held her. Held the pipe for her while she smoked. She tried everything, writhing and thrashing, but his hold was iron.

"You'll never get away from me."

She would. She'd be taken away from here, up to the heavens where he could never touch her again.

"Where are my drugs?"

She laughed, and she barely recognized the sound that came out of her. He shook her, and her head snapped back and forth. It hurt.

"Where are my fucking drugs?" He didn't raise his voice. That was Dean's thing. He always spoke quietly so you had to lean in. Coax it out of him.

"Gone."

"No way. No way you smoked all that in two days."

"I didn't smoke it, asshole. Someone stole it."

He laughed into her hair and she felt a fleck of spittle on her ear. "Bullshit."

Leaving the dogs outside, he marched her into the house, to the living room, where Sarah sat grimly on the futon with some guy. The woman sucked in her breath as Dean carried Neveah inside.

"You're both lying cunts." His tone was conversational. Almost friendly. "You lied and said she wasn't hanging around, now you're lying and saying my drugs are gone."

"I tried to use some to buy myself a ride. The asshole was bigger than me and just took it. Took all of it. Took my bag and my clothes and my phone, too."

"If this guy took her phone, you can use that to track him," Sarah said.

"I'm not so stupid that I'd give her a phone that could be traced. It's a shitty burner. Explains why you weren't answering my texts." He still held her, tight around the ribs. Each breath burned like fire.

"The drugs are gone, Dean." Neveah fought down her panic. "What now?"

He laughed and gave her a squeeze which made her yelp. "You'd better hope they're not gone."

"They're fucking gone! I told you! I'd fucking be to Boston by now if I had them."

Dean winked at Sarah. "I knew she wouldn't go to New York. My people are from there. 'S how I knew you were lying. I know this little bitch better than you ever will."

"They're gone!"

"No."

"You won't find them here because they're gone."

"If you're telling the truth, you just killed us both, sweetheart."

"How much are we talking about?" Sarah asked. "Enough to kill over?"

Depending on who you dealt with, any amount could be enough to kill over.

"Fifty grand worth."

Neveah brought a hand to her mouth. No way. No fucking way. She'd taken a bag. There were two of them in Dean's room. "Shut up. That's not possible."

He let her go. Stood up. Paced. When he finally turned and she saw his face, she could see fear inching around his eyes, and she realized he wasn't lying. "It isn't cut yet. It's pure."

The dick who stole it would have a big surprise when he took his first hit. She hoped he was ready for it. Better yet, she hoped he wasn't. Jesus, she was glad she hadn't had time with it to take a hit of her own. A mental picture of herself, lying beside the stream where the first guy left her, choking on her own puke...

"This is going to go so much easier if you just tell me

where you hid it."

"I've told you—"

Dean reached out, took her hand, and with a *snap* he broke her little finger. The room turned white, and she thought this had to be like what a nuclear blast was like, the second before everything was incinerated. Then, like a tidal wave, the pain rushed in.

Her finger was such a small part of her body. If it was going to hurt like this, couldn't she just cut it off?

The pain blared like a warning claxon, and she actually started to sweat. She curled into a little ball and clutched her hand as Dean tore the house apart. When she opened her eyes she could see Sarah, perched on the edge of the futon, hand tight over her mouth, eyes big, watching. The other man seemed uncomfortable, but didn't say anything.

Dean pulled the ash out of the woodstove, depositing it on the floor with a powdery thump. He pulled every can and every jar out of the well-stocked pantry. Every dish came out of the cupboards, even though there was no way she could have hidden fifty thousand dollars' worth of crystal meth in there. He threw them on the floor and they shattered there.

She made eye contact with Sarah, who looked away. Neveah wanted to mouth "I'm sorry," but her finger hurt too much.

Dean approached the futon. "Get up."

Sarah and the man did. He pulled a knife and slit the mattress, reaching around inside it. He slashed every pillow. Nothing.

He came back to Neveah. Took her other hand. She started to scream. To beg. She offered him everything she had, which at this point was only herself. He spat in her face and reminded her she was already his.

Then he broke the pinky on her left hand.

There was no moment of white before the pain, no calm before the storm. This time the pain slammed her like a truck, hurting everywhere from her hand to her toes to the roots of her teeth and her hair. She couldn't even wipe his spit off her face. She was nothing but tears and pain, melting into the floor.

She supposed he ransacked the bathroom and the bedroom. At this point, she didn't know, and who really cared?

Sarah did.

Pity for the woman flickered in her. As soon as Dean went into the bedroom, she came to Neveah's side, used a corner of her shirt to wipe the spit off. "Are you all right? Did he hurt you?"

A flash of red anger cut through the pain. He'd just broken both of her goddamn pinky fingers. Of course she wasn't all right. The hurt made her tongue thick and useless in her mouth, so she didn't say anything.

Sarah ran a cool hand over her forehead, and it felt good.

Neveah closed her eyes. "He's going to kill me," she whispered.

"No, he's—"

"He's going to kill both of us. We have to do something."

"What can we do?"

Uncurling herself, she sat up. She tried to rub her eyes, but no matter what she did, her dumb broken fingers seemed to get in the way. She shook her head. Sarah went into the kitchen. The man chased after her a bit.

"Sit your ass back down, Asa. I'm getting her some ibuprofen."

Asa watched.

Sarah brought four pills, and Neveah swallowed them with a glass of room temperature water. It even hurt to hold the glass, though the smooth surface felt good on her finger.

Pushing the smashing, ripping sounds from her mind, Neveah tried to figure how to get rid of Dean. Shooting him would be the most simple way. The shotgun no longer sat by the door. She hefted the pint glass in her hand, wondered if she could bring it down on his head hard enough to kill him. Or at least hard enough to knock him out so she could tie him up.

If she didn't kill him, she could humiliate him, subjugate him like he'd done to her all those years... No. Best just to kill him.

She wondered what she'd be able to do when she was nothing more than an extraterrestrial consciousness. She'd really be able to fuck with people then. Maybe if Dean came back as a ghost, she and he could square off, a battle of disembodied beings.

"Do you have anything stronger than ibuprofen?" Neveah asked. It would be beyond nice to slip away from reality right now, just a little bit.

"No. You're lucky I have those. I don't usually take anything."

Sarah'd had a problem with drinking once. Neveah could tell from the way the woman gave the info. Interesting. Her gaze fell on the fireplace poker. Iron, with a nice, thick, twisted handle. It looked heavy, like it would do some damage.

If she picked it up now, Asa would see, and he'd sound the alert. She needed to get to Dean without him realizing. Let him keep doing his search-and-destroy bullshit. She met Asa's eyes and he looked away.

That gave her an idea. She started to cry. It got Sarah's attention immediately—must have catered to the mother in her. Neveah put on her most miserable look. Sarah rushed to her side. Neveah held out her arms for a hug. Sarah complied, like she knew she would. She got her mouth in close to Sarah's ear and whispered, "Can you take care of Asa?"

The woman jerked, looked at her, and Neveah responded with a howl. "My hands hurt so bad!"

Sarah leaned back in, and whispered, "I don't know." Her breath tickled Neveah's ear and gave her goose bumps.

She shifted so she could reach Sarah's ear. "I'm going to take the fireplace poker, and I'm going into the bedroom."

"Hey," Asa said. He sounded uncertain. Apparently kidnapping and holding people hostage weren't things he typically did. "Are you whispering?"

Sarah snapped over her shoulder. "She's in pain. Can't you see that?"

Asa recoiled.

"Can you manage the poker?" the woman asked. "With your hands, I mean?"

"I don't know. I hope so. But if you don't take care of Asa, it doesn't matter."

"I'll do it."

"How?"

"I don't know."

It was obvious that Sarah wasn't accustomed to violence. She'd never specifically said so, but she'd probably never even been hit before today. It was weird to think there were really people like that out there, who weren't intimate with violence. *How would you realize you were alive without it? Wouldn't you lose touch with yourself if parts of you didn't hurt?*

She looked around the living room, for something Sarah could use against Asa. He watched them. He wore his suspicion on his face, and she bet they had moments before he shouted for Dean. "Where's the shotgun?" she whispered

"They took it."

"Took it where?"

"I don't know."

"Can you get him outside?"

"I don't *know*!" Sarah wobbled on the edge of panic.

"Calm down."

"Step away from her," Asa said, taking a half step forward.

"Kiss me," Neveah muttered.

"*What?*"

"Kiss me!"

Sarah did. Neveah peeked out from the kiss, and saw Asa's face go red. He was an old Vermonter alright, and was as unaccustomed to wanton displays of sexuality as Sarah was to violence. Neveah met his gaze, and he looked away. He made an uncomfortable noise in his throat, and studied the window.

If she were fast enough, Neveah could do both. Asa and Dean. She drained the rest of the glass of water, and held it out to Sarah. She couldn't deal with all this *and* her hands hurting. Once dark fell and the aliens came back, she wouldn't have a body any more. The pain would be gone. Forever. Like all the good parts of death without any of the bad.

Sarah went to refill the water glass without comment. She'd known Asa since they were teenagers. They'd gone to the same high school. He was a couple of years ahead of her. What did Neveah mean "get him?" She let the water run until it got nice and cold. When she started back towards the living room, and Asa glanced up at her, Neveah made her move. She lunged for the fireplace poker, wrapped her broken hands around it, and in a fluid move lunged for Asa.

Sarah wanted to scream at him to watch out, wanted to do something dramatic like drop the glass. But she didn't. She stayed silent and held the glass as Asa said "Hey." Then Neveah hit him, and he slumped like a sack of grain.

She covered her mouth with her free hand. Neveah met her eyes and brought a finger to her lips. Sarah nodded, unable to take her eyes away from how Neveah's pinky angled off to one side, broken and damaged.

The girl moved for the bedroom, stalking like a tigress.

The smell of Asa's blood reached her.

From the bedroom, there was a yelp and a crash. Dean charged out, blood streaming from a cut above his left eye. He ran at Sarah, and she acted without thinking, raising the pint glass and smashing it into the red spot above his eye. He expected neither the cold of the water or the jagged pain of the glass smashing and grinding right into the tender spot that Neveah's attack had left.

Outside, the dogs howled and barked, and clawed at the door to be let inside. Dean yowled, sounding as animal as they did, and stepped back.

Behind him, Neveah swung the poker. Sarah had time to notice bits of blood and hair stuck to it as it made miserable contact with the inside of Dean's knee. He fell to his hands and knees, and this time she hit him in the tail bone. Her swings grew weaker and weaker, and he reached for Sarah with bloody hands. She noticed his fingers were short and chubby, with blunt fingernails.

"Stop!" Sarah shouted.

"No. Not until he's dead."

"He can't walk. He can't hurt us."

Dean sobbed on the floor. A green bubble of snot formed in his nostril and popped, goo dribbling down over his lips. Tears streamed from his eyes. They mixed with the blood from his cut.

"I'm not safe so long as he's alive."

"He can't walk." Sarah went to Neveah and plucked the poker from her fingers to lay it on the floor. She gathered Neveah into her arms. The girl vibrated in her embrace like a taut guitar string. Seething.

"It's all right."

Neveah shook her head.

"We're safe."

"Can we go?" Neveah asked. "Leave here?"

It was awfully close to dark. The sun set early this time of year. The people of Wickenden would be on alert too, knowing Asa was up here... But they could do it. Get out of the mountains before full dark set upon them. She'd filled the car up on her way home Tuesday. She always filled the car on her way home. She knew someday her goal would be to get as far away as possible. She scanned the ruin of her home. Today was as good a day as any. "Let me pack a few things."

"Is there time?"

No, probably there wasn't, but she did have a few possessions she refused to leave behind. She kept some of them in a little suitcase in her bedroom, prepped for this moment like an expectant mother's hospital bag.

"I'll only be a moment." She picked up the little bag, and a sweatshirt, and a pillow. Anything else they could buy along the way.

Sarah hesitated a moment before returning to the living room. Neveah had killed Asa Gardner. Did she really want to be with someone like that? But she wasn't *with* anyone—they were fleeing an impossible situation together. Nothing more. They would arrive somewhere safe, Sarah would let her out, and Neveah would fade to a masturbatory fantasy. One day Sarah would question whether she was even real or not, if she'd ever met a girl whose name was almost heaven.

In the living room, Neveah crouched next to Dean's face.

"They're going to find you," he said. His voice was a croak.

"They'll never find me where I'm going."

"Tito's place? That's the first place anyone will look for you."

Neveah opened her mouth, then closed it again. She looked so very young in that moment. Creeping guilt sluiced over Sarah, remembering Neveah's mouth on hers. It wasn't right.

"I'm not going to Tito's."

"Where else do you got to go?"

Neveah laughed a brave little laugh. "Like I'd tell you."

"They know about Sarah's daughter in California. That's going to be the second place they look for you, after Tito's."

Sarah barged forward. "Who knows about her?"

Dean rolled his eyes towards her. It looked like it hurt, a lot. Good. In that moment she shared Neveah's wrath. If he put her baby in danger, she wanted him to hurt.

"My fucking supplier. What kind of kid did you think you were getting yourself involved with?" A bit of blood dribbled out from the corner of his mouth, and he started to cough.

"Who are they?"

"Mexicans," Neveah said. "I never officially met them, but I was around sometimes when they picked up and dropped off. They're... bad guys."

"When they see she's not with Cassie they'll leave her alone, right? They won't hurt her if Neveah's nowhere around, right?"

Hurt washed over Neveah's expression. "You'd leave me?"

"No! Of course not." If it meant keeping Cassie safe, there was a chance she might do a lot more than leave Neveah behind. The thought startled her. No. She couldn't think like these people. She could take the girl somewhere else, and leave her with friends. Or her family. Surely Neveah had a mother and a father somewhere who were worried sick about her. She imagined the tearful reunion, then saw herself joining Cassie, safe from Mexican drug dealers. "Let's go," she said.

Outside, a flood of dog greeted them. Freckles, Anansi, Loki, and the two who'd been hurt. Freya and Scrabble. Scrabble, she'd decided, was the dog who'd been poisoned. She seemed much better now, standing a little ways off from the others. Sarah hadn't thought she'd survive.

What on earth would she do with five dogs when she didn't need them to keep the things at bay? *Worry about it later.* She let them all into the car.

Neveah paused before she got in. "The tires," she said.

"What about them."

"Someone slashed them. With a screwdriver. Must have been Dean."

Dean, or Asa, or Dave, or one of the hellish things themselves. They didn't like the light, they avoided it, but she'd seen them out in it when they needed to. It weakened them, but didn't kill them. "One tire?"

The Subaru carried a full sized spare. One tire, they could handle.

"Both the ones on this side. What about the other tires in the barn?"

The question irritated her—the things in the barn were *tires* and would need to be mounted on rims to go on the car. You couldn't just take a tire swing from a tree and throw it on a vehicle. "No. They won't work. We'd need special tools to mount them."

"Can you drive on a flat?"

Sarah pondered the question while she looked around her yard. Smears of colors streaked across the sky, pinks and purples and blues. The shadows stretched long all around them. The air temperature grew cooler. She put on the sweatshirt she was carrying, and thought. Could they get to Wickenden on the spare and a flat? It would bend the rim, but probably it could physically be done.

But then what? Would there be a garage open? A night in Wickenden might not be much better than a night here.

She was a fool for not leaving sooner. What had she thought? That she could outlast them? They were cosmic and eternal, stardust made into a living creature.

Surrender. We can help. There is nothing to worry about. Worlds to discover. Stories to catalog and help with. Peace for you.

Sarah clapped her hands over her ears, but it was no use. The sound came from inside her head, not from outside. They were telepathic, on top of everything else.

And you could be as well. Could be with us. One of us. Please, Sarah, do consider it in light of the unfortunate incidences taking place at your home today. Your police will surely be curious, and is this the type of notoriety you want your daughter to have to deal with? We can solve all of it. We're happy to. Join us.

"I won't!"

"Sarah? Are you okay?"

Okay? She was about as far from okay as she could ever imagine being.

She should have left so long ago. When she first saw the tracks, first heard the whispers in the darkness. She should never have wanted to know where the voices came from. How they tied in with the things found in the river—the ones only spoken of, never photographed. Hot tears flushed down her cheeks.

What if she did give in?

Yes! Please! You'll find us to be delightful companions for you. And we can guarantee your daughter's safety.

That was worth considering.

What about Neveah? Sarah thought back at them.

The voice in her head paused. *She lacks certain qualities we look for when we choose new members of our kind.*

Sarah looked at the girl. The car separated them, the doors open. The setting sun lit her face from the side. Wide brown eyes, pert nose, high cheeks. She looked so pretty, so innocent. Could she unlearn what she was? Unlearn the drugs, and be a nice girl, evolve into a woman?

No. She cannot. You'd best leave her to the problems she's brought to your doorstep.

Sarah frowned. *People can change,* she thought. *Anyone can.*

We are not interested in her. We advise you send her on her way.

Not an option. *Yeah, well, fuck you too.*

The voice in her mind let out a disappointed sigh, and

retreated. They were alone again. It was a relief, though the sinking sun suggested they wouldn't be alone for long.

"Are you okay?" Neveah stood at her side now, reaching out with a poor, mutilated hand.

"I'm okay." Sarah's voice quavered. She felt pity for the girl... They didn't want her. She snapped herself out of it. It wasn't pity. She was jealous. She *wished* they didn't want her. "Let's go back in the house."

"What are we going to do with Dean?" Sometimes Neveah seemed worldly and mature, other times she reminded her of her freshmen lit students, wide eyed, away from home for the first time.

Sarah let the dogs out of the car. They poured out, and she corralled them back to the house. Inside, Dean raised his head. The dogs avoided him, eyed him warily. They circled, agitated by the smell of blood. "Help me." His voice rattled, like there was fluid in his lungs. "Nev, please. We been through so much together, you and me. You can't leave me like this."

"Help me with him," Neveah said.

A chill inched down Sarah's spine. "Help you what?"

"I want to move him onto the couch. He'll be more comfortable there."

Did they want him comfortable? What were they going to do with him? Another thought came to her. Did he have a car?

Neveah tried to lift him, but her hands hurt her too badly. Sarah wanted to do that to *his* thick fingers. Instead, she lifted him herself. He seemed reduced, less than he had been. His legs dangled uselessly as she moved him. He blinked up at her with unfocused eyes in his pale face. He wasn't going to make it.

Asa lay slumped on the floor next to the futon.

Sarah went to the kitchen. "Does he have a car?" she whispered.

"Yeah."

"Do you know where it is?"

"No, but I bet it's somewhere close."

Sarah nodded. They didn't walk all the way up here."

"So we go for his car!" Neveah sounded excited. "And we get out before dark?"

Fuck. Neveah racked her brain, trying to come up with a reason to stay. But the idea of five dogs inside Dean Acevedo's Honda Prelude was good. He would rather die than allow such a thing. He'd never allow her or Sarah to drive it, either.

"Go find out where he's parked it," Sarah said.

"Me?"

"You know him. He'll tell you."

"What if they took the other guy's car?"

"Then he'll know where it's parked. They came together."

Neveah bit her lip. "Okay."

She got herself a glass of water and went to Dean. He opened his eyes and flinched when he saw it in her hand. She kept her smile inside. His left pupil was dilated, big and black, the other one a pin prick. She brought the glass to his lips, which were red with blood. He looked like a boy who'd been playing with mommy's lipstick.

Stroking his hair, she asked, "Did you drive here?"

"No. Asa."

"Where's his car?"

"Not going to tell you unless you promise to take me with you."

"I promise, baby."

"You're crazy."

Why do you think that is? she wanted to ask. *Could it have to do with the fact you purchased me when I was seventeen?*

Somewhere in his skeezy Rutland apartment there was a bill of sale, and she was the property. Sometimes Dean liked to show it to her when he hit her.

"Where's the car, baby?" she asked again, her lips close

to his ear. He tried to pull away, but he was too weak. "Where's the car?"

She didn't even want the fucking car. What she wanted was for the afternoon to hurry the fuck up, and for the darkness, and for the things to come back. She glanced over at Sarah.

The woman shrugged. "We could get Asa's keys and just start walking. It might be down at Dave's place."

"Dean. Is the car at Dave's?"

He looked away with his mismatched eyes. She took his hand. Held his little finger. His eyes went wide with terror.

"Dave's place?"

He started to cry again. Blubbering. She couldn't even make out what he was saying. His finger was harder to break than she'd expected, much harder than he'd made hers look. That it took her three tries made her angry. He screamed, a low, throaty howl, and he thrashed his torso on the futon.

His legs didn't move. She must have gotten him good with the poker to the lower back. *So sorry, Dean.* She wondered if his cock still worked. Wouldn't that be a fitting end for a pimp? She whispered the question in his ear, and he started to cry even harder.

"Neveah, that's enough. We'll just take the keys from both of them and walk until we find a car."

"Or it gets dark?"

"No, we have to head back to the house before it gets dark. I'm not going to put myself or the dogs out there with those things. Or you, for that matter."

Neveah would do her best to make sure that didn't happen, and they did, in fact, wind up out there in the dark with those things. Her salvation.

When she reached into Dean's pocket, she did a little more groping around than was strictly necessary. He shook with fear.

Sarah grabbed Asa's keys and stood by the door.

"Do you like that?" she asked him. "Do you like being afraid? That's how I feel. That's how Sierra's going to feel when she gets it through her thick head that you're not actually her boyfriend." Being a commodity with sales papers was almost a blessing. At least she wasn't in Sierra's shoes. Neveah remembered the expression on Sierra's face the first time Dean had asked her to "help him out" with a friend of his. It was like she didn't get that he'd sold her services. She got it now, but wouldn't admit it.

Sierra's name made Dean cry harder, and something around his eyes softened.

"You like her?" The idea made her angry. She blinked down at him, searching for something else to do that would hurt him.

But Sarah called her name.

"Saved by the bell," she said.

He just blinked at her, stupid. Fuck him. She hurried out after Sarah and looked up at the fall sky, the first purples of dusk creeping in on the blue above. "Are you sure we'll make it to the car?"

Sarah followed her gaze, up above. "No. But we have to try."

"Wouldn't it be better to wait until tomorrow?"

The woman hesitated a moment. "No."

So they went. Each step hurt her fingers. They were a dull throb now, pain yowling at her as she moved. What more could he possibly want to take from her? He had her dignity, her body—now he'd broken two of her bones? Before he'd always been careful not to leave too many marks. Most of her customers didn't like that. But lately... He'd seemed so mad at her.

Whatever.

Sarah rushed them down the gravel drive, to the road, then west. When they found it, the cut tree smelled sweet in the fall air, and she could almost imagine cooking hotdogs over a fall bonfire. At least, she assumed that's what people did in the fall with bonfires. What did she know?

One of the dogs started to growl.

"I named them," Sarah said, out of the blue.

"Awesome."

The woman told her their names, but she forgot them all.

"Loki's growling. We have to go back."

"How much farther is it? We can make it?"

Sarah frowned. "I think it was Dave's hand I shot off last night."

So? "Why are all your neighbors ganged up with these

things?"

"They took Dave's wife."

And I'm next. As soon as it gets dark out. She hoped to hear the buzzing voice in her mind, but she met only silence. They'd learn their lesson.

"Why's he on their side if they took his wife?"

"She was a scientist. They took her."

"They like smart people, huh. You're super smart."

Sarah frowned at her. "Yeah. They're looking for people they think they can use. Who will help their civilization."

"I wonder what I can do for them."

Sarah's frown deepened. "Let's hope we never find out."

You wouldn't say that if you had a cartel of fucking Mexicans on your ass. She'd figured they'd go after Dean if they went after anyone. Didn't realize how easily he would find her, or that he'd be dead so quickly. He wasn't actually dead, of course, but it was obviously only a matter of time. He wasn't going to survive the night.

Neveah tried a question. "You ever think about letting them take you?"

"No."

"Not even a little? Like, to wonder what it feels like?"

"They had to dump Dave's wife's body somewhere. Under the woodpile. And I keep wondering if they didn't just kill her. I mean, how are we to know they got her... Her soul out."

"Consciousness," Neveah said.

"Huh?"

"Not a soul. They're probably all sciencey, if they're taking smart people. I bet they don't have a god, or care about our god. I bet they want consciousnesses."

"We have to go back." Sarah stopped walking. "Really. It's getting too late, and if they catch us out here..."

"They'll take us?"

"Or more likely kill us."

"They didn't kill Dave when they took his wife, did they?"

Sarah started walking up the hill. She whistled, and three of the dogs joined her.

"But we're almost there... Aren't we?" Neveah asked. Sarah didn't pause. She'd got them this far. Now Neveah's job was to slow the woman down as best she could. She lagged back, then dropped to the ground, clutching her ankle as best she could, with her fingers in the condition they were in.

She focused on the pain of her fingers, channeled it all into her ankle, and yowled. "I fell!"

Sarah rushed to her side and scooped her up in big, strong arms, crushing her to her massive bosom. "I've got you." The words made Neveah cringe, and Sarah felt it. "Are you all right? Did I hurt you?"

"I feel so safe with you." She leaned into Sarah's neck. The other woman didn't smell good, but Neveah couldn't imagine that she smelled like a peach herself either. She nuzzled in, and the woman held her tighter.

"I think I sprained my ankle."

"It's all right. You're light as a feather."

Fuck. She'd barely slowed them down at all. If she'd stayed walking, she could have done more. She cuddled in and willed herself to think. She needed them out here, outside, when dark fell.

"My grandparents lived here when I was a little girl." Walking and carrying Neveah barely got Sarah out of breath. Neveah guessed it made her feel good to do this confessional thing. She let her speak.

"My parents lived in Essex—up near Burlington. My father died when I was ten, and after I graduated from high school, my mother moved back here with her parents."

Big deal. I never met my father, and my stepfather sold me to a pimp.

"I can't bear the thought of leaving this place. So much history. I can't imagine a time without it. There wasn't a time without it."

"I'm sorry." She didn't know what else to say. She was never good when people were upset.

"Watching Dean tear everything apart just about broke my heart."

Neveah wondered what it was like, having a heart to break.

They turned down the long driveway, the now familiar stream at their side. The dogs drew in closer. The shadows grew darker and darker, began to merge and multiply. Neveah willed for them to slow down, for Sarah's sturdy stride to falter.

It didn't. It never would. Fuck.

One of the dogs peeled off from the pack and ran, sprinting into the darkness. She wasn't sure, but thought it was the one who'd been poisoned.

"Scrabble!"

What stupid dog names. What was a low key? And Scrabble? The game? Fuck.

She wondered if Dean were dead yet. What a small blessing that would be, not having to listen to his whining.

"One more night," Sarah said. "We'll lock up tight and sleep it through. I wonder if there's time to put Asa out."

"And Dean?"

"If he's dead. I think you hurt him real bad."

Sarah's words stabbed at her. *She* hurt *him*? What did Sarah think she was, some kind of awful monster? She was defending herself. The asshole was holding them hostage. She wanted to be put down, wanted to not be carried. She wished she hadn't come up with the dumb thing of pretending to twist her ankle. She actually thought they were moving faster now because of it.

"I think my ankle's okay," she muttered.

"It's all right. We're almost back."

No! She didn't want to be back. She started to twist and thrash a bit, so the woman put her down. Sarah's reproachful gaze didn't make her less angry. Everyone against her. Fuck them all. Looking away, she pretended to put weight on the ankle. She tested it out and carried on with a feigned limp.

"I'm trying to help you."

"Thanks," Neveah mumbled over her shoulder. She caught a glimpse of Sarah, whose face fell.

17 – DARKNESS

Sarah couldn't figure out what was up with Neveah. Her limp wasn't right, leading her to wonder if she'd ever actually hurt it at all. She was so light, carrying her hadn't been much of a trial... But she didn't seem to appreciate the gesture. Some people have a hard time asking for help, she reasoned. Even so, something was off.

They would weather one more night in the cabin, then in the morning they'd strike out for the cars. She'd spent plenty of nights here. One more wouldn't be the end of her. They were so close... The sky overhead transformed from rose to purple, and from the east, deep navy, speckled with stars, encroached on the horizon.

Sarah hurried. She called to Scrabble again. What was the use, really? She'd never bothered to name them before, so why did she suddenly expect they would learn? Freckles drew close, almost tripping her. Neveah had abandoned her limp— must have been a fleeting thing, not really a sprain or a twist at all, maybe one of those sudden, shooting pains which comes and goes.

There, with darkness falling, and god knew what about to slink out of the bushes and attack them, Sarah found herself making excuses for the girl. It didn't make for a very promising start.

There is no start, she told herself. *She's a hitchhiker. She's going to Boston. You're going to California. End of story.* She forced herself to try to imagine coming home to Neveah after a hard day of work. Neveah making her soup when she was sick. Neveah buying her flowers just because.

We have the power to remove these trials. Join us.

"No!" She realized, as she shouted, that she'd spoken aloud, and not in the confines of her mind.

Neveah turned.

"Run! They're close!" Sarah shouted.

The girl stopped. Maybe she'd misunderstood. Sarah grabbed her arm and half carried her up the porch steps and into the cabin. One, two, three, four dogs squirted in around them, and she slammed the door, bashed the wooden bar into place. "Go check the windows!"

"I don't think so." Neveah's tone had gone cold.

"Go check the windows!" Maybe the girl hadn't heard her.

Neveah didn't move. It didn't matter, she'd done this alone plenty of times. Never with this little time to spare maybe, but she'd made it just fine without anyone's help.

Something heavy thumped against the door, startling her. The living room windows were all right, she needed to look in the bedroom and the bathroom. She ran. The bathroom window hung open. She caught a glimpse of blackness through the glass, a few bare branches caught in the light from the house. She slammed and locked them, and without giving herself time to celebrate, rushed to the bedroom. One of the windows gaped open, and the sudden certainty gripped her that *something* was in the house with her. Better to shut it in and deal with it than risk more of them getting inside. She slammed the window, panting. Sweating. She wiped at her forehead, stinging sweat rolling into her eyes. Her heart beat a frantic tattoo in her chest.

In the living room, the dogs stopped barking all at once, like a switch had been turned off. Cool dread sluiced down her back, freezing the sweat there.

She'd been so selfish. Keeping the dogs for protection, no thought of their needs. And now? She forced herself out of the daze and hurried to the living room.

The door hung open, beckoning towards the darkness beyond. A shape filled it, alien, buzzing, all useless wings and mandibles. The dogs were gone.

Dean stared from his place on the couch, eyes wide and terrified. Sarah saw the very last vestiges of sanity leaking away as he looked at the thing. What was left behind was a slavering, mortally wounded shell of a man.

Maybe he deserved it.

Did anyone deserve this?

"I'm ready," Neveah said.

For a crazy half-second, Sarah thought the girl was talking to her. Ready for what? They couldn't leave until morning. The things wouldn't let them out of the house. The only way out tonight was up and up and up, but you'd have to leave your body behind.

Then she realized that the girl focused on the monstrosity before her. Imploring it.

It reached out with a segmented leg covered in bristling, sensile hairs, and swatted her aside. She landed on top of Dean. He groaned, no longer able to even cry out.

Join us.

"I won't."

Something in Neveah's face changed. She looked the same as she had when Sarah had stopped her from tormenting Dean. Hurt masked with nasty anger.

The shotgun was past the futon. Could she make it in time? It was vital to get the door closed. She didn't know how many of them were in these Vermont hills, doing their experiments, looking for minerals, but she knew she didn't have a hope to fight off more than one at a time.

We'll not harm the dogs if you come easily.

"You have the dogs?"

Neveah's glare thickened. It was as though she were jealous, if she wanted to be a part of this.

The dogs ran into the night, afraid. We can catch them, or we can let them be.

Would this be how they wore her down? The dogs? She'd thought of them as tools for almost two months. Freckles and Loki were new—there'd been two before them who met bitter ends thanks to the creatures. She glanced at Neveah.

Perhaps we'll start with harming your friend.

"I'm so sorry," Sarah said to her.

The girl glared back. "Tell them to take me. To take me to space with them."

She didn't know what she was asking. "I never should have picked you up." If Sarah hadn't intervened, Neveah would have passed through the mountains undisturbed.

Dean let out a ghostly moan.

Tonight it ends, dear Sarah. You'll not come with us?

Cassie's face wavered in her mind. She couldn't. Not

even to save the dogs. Besides, if the thing went after Neveah, perhaps it would give her time to get to the shotgun. "They don't matter to me."

You're lying.

"Do what you must."

The thing swiveled its faceless head towards Neveah. Her eyes went wide as it started for her.

Sarah ran for the gun while the thing lunged for the girl. She jumped back, over the futon, and the creature descended on Dean. It reached out with a pair of pincers. Grasping him, it twisted and pulled and, with a soft groan, he came apart in its clawed hands, and all Sarah could think of was a gross caricature of a person eating a lobster drenched in butter. This time, though, the lobster did the dipping, did the twisting and pulling, and it was the human who was torn apart. The attack spattered the futon with gore and blood. It made a steady dripping sound as it pattered onto the floor. The stench of blood made her recoil, made the little hairs stand at attention on the back of her neck.

Neveah screamed and didn't stop.

Picking up the loaded shotgun, Sarah pumped it once, and aimed it at the creature. The sight of Dean and all the blood made her hands shake. When she pulled the trigger, only a bit of the buckshot hit the creature. It turned its head, fixing its wavering tentacles at her. Then it hissed, and flexed its wings in her direction.

Half of the tentacles seemed to writhe to consider Neveah, half Sarah. Her hands shook as she reloaded the shotgun. She willed Neveah to just *stop*, but couldn't pay any attention to her.

You are making a grave mistake. The voice buzzed and rattled in every corner of her mind. Neveah shut up with a whimper.

"Get out of my head!" She screamed, raising the gun.

"No!" Neveah's shout startled her. The creature moved as she fired. Her shot went wild, the gun kicking into her shoulder.

The buzzing seemed to convey regret as the creature skittered towards her on all those legs, tentacles writhing. The wings, impotent, fluttered behind it.

She'd heard people talk about their lives flashing before

their eyes. As the thing crossed the small living room and she fumbled to reload, she wondered what space would have been like. Wondered if Cassie would be all right. Wondered why life had been so cruel to Neveah to make her into such a hateful, sour young woman.

The thing descended on Sarah, pincers digging into her. Now she was the lobster dinner. The gun dropped from her hands and she reached into the mass of tentacles, taking fistfuls and pulling at them. They surged, thick and prehensile in her hands, but the creature recoiled and thrashed. She was hurting it.

"Stop it! Stop it!" Neveah shouted. She came from behind the futon, brandishing a floor lamp at the thing. She extended it, hit the thing with it, smashing the spiral light bulb over its head.

It screamed and thrashed, its pain disproportional to the feeble hit. *Must be the mercury*, Sarah had time to think.

Then the thing flexed and spasmed, and Sarah felt a curious tugging sensation a beat before pain exploded throughout her body.

It cut it's so sharp. Her thoughts were so disjointed, they reminded her of the creature's buzzing cadence.

She reached for herself, trying to put herself back together again, but her hands came away thick, and it was getting dark—probably because the lamp went out.

No. Dark for other reasons, but she couldn't figure out why because it was getting dark—no, that wasn't quite right.

She thought there probably should have been a tunnel. It didn't seem right there wasn't one. A tunnel, a light, a something. Anything but this dark.

She hoped maybe they were taking her to space after all, but she knew she'd been cut too deeply. Things weren't right in her body. The blood on her hands was brilliant and slippery and somehow she knew it was that peculiar color because it came from her heart.

She wondered if the dogs would be all right.

About the Author

If it screams, squelches, or bleeds, Kristin Dearborn has probably written about it. Kristin has written books such as *Sacrifice Island* (DarkFuse), *Trinity* (DarkFuse), and had fiction published in several magazines and anthologies. *Stolen Away* was recently a limited edition offered from Thunderstorm Books, which sold out.

She revels in comments like "But you look so normal...how do you come up with that stuff?" A life-long New Englander, she aspires to the footsteps of the local masters, Messrs. King and Lovecraft. When not writing or rotting her brain with cheesy horror flicks (preferably creature features!) she can be found scaling rock cliffs or zipping around Vermont on a motorcycle, or gallivanting around the globe. Kristin's latest DarkFuse release is *Woman in White*.

Find more about Kristin online at kristindearborn.com or Facebook.

ALSO FROM
LOVECRAFT EZINE PRESS

The King in Yellow Tales volume I, by Joseph S. Pulver, Sr.

The Sea of Ash, by Scott Thomas

The Lurking Chronology, by Pete Rawlik

Autumn Cthulhu, edited by Mike Davis

Nightmare's Disciple, by Joseph S. Pulver, Sr.

www.ingramcontent.com/pod-product-compliance
Lightning Source LLC
Chambersburg PA
CBHW020632130626
46552CB00003B/1190